D1446429

BY

David Boyle

Arctic Wolf Publishing

Blood Works
All Rights Reserved
Copyright © 2008 David Boyle
Second Edition 2009

Arctic Wolf Publishing
http://www.arcticwolfpublishing.com
ISBN - 10: 0-9802197-5-2
ISBN - 13: 978-0-9802197-5-3

Dedication/Acknowledgment

First and foremost, I would like to thank Arctic Wolf Publishing for this once in a lifetime opportunity. I am forever beholden to him for discovering something in my fiction, and then giving me the chance to share my vision with the world. I have fulfilled a dream because of this wonderful break, and it's one that I will never take for granted. Words can't express my gratitude to you.

I want to send out my heartfelt appreciation to the world of horror authors that started it all, and that continue to pave the way. Each and every one of them inspires me. It is my good fortune and privilege to be in their company.

I would like to dedicate this anthology to horror readers around the world. Without them, this book could not breathe.

I want to thank my wonderful wife Elizabeth for being the pillar of strength and wisdom at my side, for always believing in me, and for her undying love.

I also want to thank my family for their encouragement and enthusiasm: my brothers, Al and Rich, and my parents, Allan and Geri. And a special thank you to my dear friend Ed Minus for helping to make me a better writer and for teaching me the depth and value of language. I don't know where I'd be without him in my corner. He is a literary genius.

Last, but certainly not least, I want to thank all of my friends that never stopped supporting me even when their lives were in overload. You are amazing people.

BLOOD WORKS

CONTENTS:

Bad Connection

H is life was turned upside down without warning. He was devastated. She invited him over that night and then a tidal wave hit him that rocked his world. He never saw it coming. No one ever sees it coming. That's just the way women operate, he thought. How was he supposed to deal with that type of heartbreak, so unforeseen and dramatic? He felt like he had been knocked to the floor and was on his knees, trying to pick up the pieces. But there were too many. Was his life shattered beyond repair? Rejection was not something he was well-prepared for. He felt like a bomb had been dropped on him. He was only weeks from asking for her hand in marriage and then she betrayed him, made a fool of him.

"I'm so sorry, Darren. I just can't." His eyes widened. His pallor faded into a ghostly white and he threw is hands into the air in disbelief. Scorned. "Two years together and you throw in the towel. What's wrong with you!?"

Her voice broke. Her words dribbled out between shaking lips. "I didn't mean for this to happen. I swear. I… I… I wish things were different."

He stared at the wall trying to stifle the rising anger. He felt the life drain out of him as he listened to a woman who once was warm and loving talk so absurdly. His world was splitting at the seams. He pinched his eyes closed. He felt weak, ashamed, embarrassed.

"How could you do this? What didn't— What

don't I do for you?"

"It's not that simple, Dar—"

Darren came apart. He pointed his finger in her face. His hand shook with anger.

"Don't give me that crap, Melissa. Of course it is! Do you have an ounce of decency? Hell, if that's what you always wanted, why string me along? Do you get off on it or something?"

A tear traveled slowly down her cheek and fell from her chin. Her eyes grew moist. He could see that her uncontrollable emotions threatened to drown her. She looked ridden with sadness, relief, and confusion all at once. But despite the obvious burning in her soul, she was clearly determined to let him go. "No! It just happened. It wasn't planned. I never meant to hurt you!"

He punched the wall and she stood by stiffly and watched. She was staggered by his outburst. It was a side of him he had kept hidden until now. Her palms cupped her face. He looked down at his bleeding knuckles and then lifted his eyes without raising his head. "That's what they all say, Melissa. Fuck it then! Enjoy yourself. I hope you're happy with whoever he is!"

Darren walked toward the door a beaten man. The look in his eyes made her uneasy. She wanted to soften the blow but it was too late. "I hope you understand one day. I didn't want it to end like this."

She stepped cautiously toward him and he extended his hand, palm up. She froze, and his disposition frightened her. A menacing facial expression singed her.

"It's a long way from over, Melissa. Mark…My…Words."

"But Darren—"

He stormed out of the room and slammed the door shut.

He eventually skipped town and found work with the cable company. His job was to travel from house to house doing repairs and modifications. That kept him busy and helped put a roof over his head. He had avoided any contact with family, friends, and relatives. He tried to date a few times but his efforts failed miserably. Something had changed inside him. A switch was flicked. One young lady, who he went out with a few times, experienced his many unresolved issues firsthand. She said he had a temper, that little things set him off. She recalled how they would sit across from each other and he would just look out into space in silence.

The woman had used her only alternative. She broke away from him. Darren forbade any and all women from getting too comfortable in his presence. Their sole purpose was to fulfill his needs, when and if he desired. He wanted the internal suffering to cease. It would not let go. It would not relent.

A year had passed since Melissa ruined him. He still was unable to purge the thoughts of her from his mind. Once, when he began to recover, when his ex was a memory and nothing more and the emotional wounds were sealing, he had finally felt himself slipping out of the dark hole. Then everything went terribly wrong: Melissa called him out of the blue. Darren tried to ignore his feelings, suppress them. But he couldn't hang up the phone. The longer they spoke the more bitter he became. She had an old friend look him up.

Why is she doing this to me? he wondered. What is her angle? What is the point? Did she enjoy smearing her new life in his face, flaunting how happy she was without him? Melissa didn't realize what she had started. Reaching out to him only pushed him closer to the edge.

He made a pact with himself that day; that somebody would feel the pain that had ravaged him since their separation, the unsavory feelings of loneliness and humiliation. Soon he would even the

7

score. Darren searched for victims who had what he wanted. Then it suddenly hit him: The unsuspecting targets were right in front of him.

His feet were propped up on a large, bulky toolbox filled with all the supplies of a cable installer: pliers, vice grips, screwdrivers, crimping tools, wire cutters and coaxial wire strippers. He sat on a plastic bucket spitting wads of chewing tobacco laden phlegm into an empty cup. His khaki pants were stained all over and there were holes in the knees. His button up work shirt was the only garment in decent condition except for the name patch— it dangled above the left breast pocket and was curled up and crinkled. The frayed strings that once bound it to the cloth were loose and frayed. The top two buttons of his shirt were undone and his clumpy chest hair was exposed. His appearance was sub-standard and the company warned him about it. He was handsome and well-kempt when he began with *Cable King*, slim and clean-cut. Now his appearance and his persona were deteriorating rapidly.

Darren no longer cared about himself or others. His remaining shreds of humanity had been stripped away a long time ago and his instability was worsening. He had slipped up horribly awhile back. But it went unnoticed, undetected. That was only the beginning. He remembered that the clock on the dash had ten minutes to five. Darren's day ended at five, sharp. Dispatch called in a few minutes ago and ordered him to Overlook Trail. A lady reported that her channels were all static. The boss told him to get a move on it.

He had no desire to take the run. He was ready to call it a day. His boss warned him he was on thin ice and if he didn't get going he could pack up his shit; effective immediately. Man did that fire him up. He whipped the cup down onto the street and tobacco juice flew everywhere.

After loading the tool box he slammed the sliding van door shut and got behind the wheel and sat there, staring into space again. The windshield was etched with dirty finger marks and various cracks were spreading. Some began small but from neglect had flared up and made deep trails in the glass. He was hypnotized by the deterioration. It was as though it all had some subliminal meaning. He grasped the wheel and rolled his grease-covered hands back and forth. He put the van in gear and spun the tires leaving a funnel of smoke in his wake.

Earlier in the day the sun was strong and blazing hot. Now it was shrouded by clouds. A thunderstorm loomed on the horizon. The van crept down Connor Street, and as he closed in on Overlook he recalled his last visit there so vividly that he could see the details as if they were on a screen before him: it was a customer at number eighteen he remembered.

She was the first victim, the first part of his revenge. The customer's daughter was home that morning. She was a gorgeous teenager. The parents were always off in some other far away place on business. At least that's what the back-up driver, Clifford, told him, unwittingly. Cliff normally serviced the area and had a reputation with the ladies. Cliffy, as the women liked to refer to him, probably scored with half the block and it flew under the radar. If anyone knew about it they sure as hell didn't give a crap. But the boys in the yard were well-aware that he did not service only their cable woes.

The teenager's parents were in Tokyo for about a week. Darren went in the house and saw a display of family photos sitting above the fireplace. He wanted them all to bleed right away; each and every one of them, especially her, their little daughter, the one in the photo; the one that answered the door. In the picture her hands wrapped around the wheel of a yacht pretending to steer while her parents watched with smiles on their faces, as if she'd done something remarkable. Soon she would do something worth praising, *in his mind*. He'd get off on sending them a picture, maybe even a video of him popping her cherry, if it wasn't spoiled already. The thoughts that entered his mind were dangerous and demented. He saw a spoiled bitch who got whatever her heart desired for being daddy's little princess. Darren looked back on the plans he had, that Melissa was supposed to be part of, when he figured she was in it for the long haul, forever. Then she cut him loose. The dreadful past was resurfacing, burning him.

He stared at the picture longer, in a daze. The parents in their forties, he guessed. The husband was a dork with a hot wife; so typical, so undeserving. They stood on the yacht with other wealthy vermin. It all made him sick. Oh…how he wanted to violate this family somehow. That little tramp traipsing around the house in the skimpy outfit was a nice start. This family needed darkness in their perfect life. He grew angrier and she was the tease, answering the door in a bathing suit, belly shirt, and pumps that gave lurid instructions to his penis; made it do bad things. That father of hers would have a stroke if he knew the way she pranced around the house in front of strangers. *Don't worry, sir. I'll take care of your naughty little girl for you while you're away.*

It was time for her lesson, but when he finished the job the girl was nowhere to be found. So he went looking for her. He rudely browsed the first floor on the prowl for that teenage meat. Nothing was off limits in his mind, and if the need arose he always was able to talk himself out of a jam.

"All done here young lady, where are you?" he yelled out. That was his best impression of a charming professional. It never failed him. His voice filled the long corridor heading toward the bedrooms where he roamed freely. He passed a bathroom on the left and the scent of her perfume drifted up his nostrils, making him crave her delicate skin. The odor was sweet and intoxicating. He imagined how her soft flesh would feel in his grasp.

At the end of the hall on the right he saw the entryway to the attic.

"Hello! Young lady, are you here?"

Her mousy voice answered from up top. "Coming, be right down!"

He walked toward the foot of the ladder and heard the sound of boxes being shuffled around. She was so involved that she didn't hear the sound of him switching on the attic fan, creating a disturbance, something that would drown out any screaming for help. Darren started to climb the wooden planks when the girl came to the top of the stairs on her way out. Darren's eyes held tight on hers. Her face wrinkled with suspicion. He spoke convincingly. "I'm coming up. I have to check the box up there with these wires. A little troubleshooting has to be done. Then I'm on my way."

She tried to descend the stairs but he crowded them and blocked any access she considered for a getaway.

"It'll only take a second, relax." At the top he stepped forward and pulled the trap door shut behind him. Suddenly it hit her. She was in a world of danger.

"I better go. I need to check on something," she said, her response shaky with alarm and desperation.

"I'm not going to hurt you, Felicia."

She folded her arms in front of her chest nervously. Her eyes scouted every corner looking for an escape route. Darren inched toward her with his hands raised laterally at the shoulders, acting innocent, benign. The look in his eyes was devious, sinister. He leered at her, wanted her. Felicia had Melissa's piercing green eyes and boyish dimples. An erection formed in his pants. She turned her head away from his mangy face. She was afraid to ask the questions that were swimming on the tip of her tongue: How do you know my name? What do you want?

She asked anyway. He scowled. He was

peeved by her questions. Why couldn't she just let nature take its course, allow things to shape themselves?

"It won't matter in a few seconds, girly." He approached her and stood, brooding over her from a foot away. Felicia stiffened. She had nowhere to run. No weapon. She considered kneeing him in the nuts and then reconsidered her defense. It better knock him down, she thought. He was big. He towered over her. He would overpower her. She was no match for his brawn. Only a *perfect* strike, a small window of time, would allow her to get past him and down the stairs to safety. Felicia faced the truth. It was a long-shot to out-maneuver him and get to freedom. Her feet shuffled fearfully on the floor as he closed the gap between them. The floor-boards creaked and jiggled underneath his heavy frame. She wanted to scream. But she knew one false move, one foolish utterance, would endanger her more than the horrible act he was about to commit.

"Cooperate, and you live. You can do that, can't you?" He lifted his arm and stroked her hair with his filthy hand. "Goood girl."

She shuddered and closed her eyes. She smelled the nauseating stench of his body. Her head twitched at the touch of his clammy hand sliding under the curls of her hair. A fountain of vomit rose from her stomach and snaked its way to her throat.

It was repulsive for her to watch his tongue worm out of his mouth and wet his lips. His eyes glazed over like he was in heat. She choked back the urge to scream. She kept bullshitting herself.

It'll be over soon. It'll be over soon. Don't do anything stupid. I hope I wake up soon if this is a nightmare.

Darren was ready to do vile things to her, fulfill every grotesque sexual desire with her; then kill her. His actions were her choosing. Her life was in her own hands. He slipped his hand down her shorts and she fought back the flood of tears that wanted to be released.

That day always put a smile on his face, made him feel better every time, like a new man. At his will his mind rewound itself and retraced the sweltering fifteen minutes in that attic. His dominance over her aroused him. He knew she would never speak of it again. He owned her then and still now. If the incident ever leaked from her lips, if she ever broke her silence, he promised pain, and not just to her. She was wise to surrender to him. He even called her Melissa during his huffing and puffing, forced her to beg for more. When it was all done he confronted a deeper knowledge of himself: Once wasn't enough, he craved another victim.

The sky warned of a storm drawing closer, clouds overspreading. The breeze nudged stronger. Small flashes of lighting drew more energy. Darren turned onto the street. The address given was number sixty-three Overlook. The van crawled down the long roadway. The street was crowded with trees, deep woods between and behind many residences. Ahead was a mailbox with number forty-seven stenciled on it.

He put the radio on to WHYK. The station broadcasted the weather for the next forty-eight hours and forecasted heavy downpours through the evening, more on the way tomorrow. He passed number fifty-five.

The street was quiet, nobody outdoors. No kids playing or screaming in the back yards. A majority of the families were off on vacations or out of town for the weekend. He smirked at the lush landscapes, the manicured lawns, driveways that could accommodate a fleet of cars with room to spare. A road full of suburban sprawl and wives looking for something to fill the boredom, besides spending their husband's cash and screwing delivery men to fill the void in their lives.

Finally, he arrived at an enormous brick home

and pulled into the driveway. A wooden sign read sixty-three. It hung over the three-car garage, tacked onto the vinyl siding. He parked next to a privacy screen of cedar trees that were deep green and had pointed tops. Both sides of the driveway were planted with long rows of the showy evergreens clustered together to hide the driveway from plain view. Darren clipped a badge to his shirt pocket and got out of the truck with a baseball cap in his hand. He sauntered up the driveway to the front door and placed the cap backwards on his head. His sweaty hair was practically glued to his forehead. He climbed the brick stairs and saw the doorbell glowing, the surrounding encasement read *Bless Our Home and All Who Enter.*

He pushed it. Moments later a tall brunette answered the door and again he thought of Melissa.

This one had some of her characteristics: the eyes, the hair, the posture; he was turned on by this woman and at the same time imagined drowning her in the pool he saw in the back yard when he pulled in. Watching her fight for air, maybe pull her head to the surface for a quick, elusive breath— then shove it under again. She was dressed in Capri pants with a pink tank-top that showed off her sexy bronzed skin. He despised her instantly and wondered how much time she wasted on herself and nothing else? *Fucking whore* were the words that came to mind. He wanted to yell it in her face at the top of his lungs, but he turned on the charm so she would let him in.

"Hi Miss, here from Cable King. I'm here to fix... uh?" Darren feigned professionalism by consulting his clipboard: "Static problems."

He entered the house and stood in the foyer.

"If you have any questions during my visit..." He flicked at his badge with his finger. "My name's Darren."

The lady had a fire in her eyes, a brewing anger, or perhaps repulsion raised her brow. She was clearly turned off by his appearance and did a poor job of hiding it. His badge was tarnished and she only could read the name *Beckwith*. The letter D was barely visible at the top. The name tag on the opposite side was curled and illegible, without his picture. And she didn't wonder why either. She did wonder, however, who one earth would hire such a slob to go on a call all dirty and haggard. It appeared as though he'd spent the day putting on a roof, not installing cable.

He smiled, and a set of dingy crooked teeth greeted her. "Point me to the problem and I'll get started," he demanded.

She guided him to a family room. A huge television in front of a wide wall was surrounded with racks of videos and a stereo mounted atop. Behind the wall was a kitchen the lady disappeared into. The set emitted static and the noise filled the room. He lowered the volume and went to work. Darren tinkered behind the set. While he worked he scanned the layout of the house and made mental note of the details. She was *alone* in the house. A cat was curled up in a ball on top of a love-seat. No sign of a dog. An alarm box on the wall near the front door looked easy to disarm. He smiled.

The lady was in the kitchen babbling with her

husband on the phone. Darren eavesdropped. Her voice echoed and he heard it from where he worked in the family room. He pulled a couple wires from the back of the set and hooked them to his belt loop. He removed the roll of fresh cable from his tool box and unrolled what he needed for the repair. His hands operated with precision. His face tightened with an unbreakable concentration, like that of a skilled surgeon performing a tense procedure. He heard the chatter in the kitchen, louder now.

"I miss you too. How are the kids?"

"Good. Send them my love."

"When will you be home?"

"Afternoon is perfect. I know, right? We'll put the kids to bed early."

Her tone faded to a whisper.

The phone conversation made him insane. He was stripping the new cable prior to attachment. The incisors on the pliers gouged his finger. Blood seeped from his thumb and he licked off the oozing streams before they hit the floor. The lady giggled in the other room.

"Say hi to your sister for me. Love you too, bye."

She was on her way to the kitchen doorway when Darren entered first with a handful of coaxial cable. He held it up for her to see. "Just a few bad wires, you're all set."

She saw the blood stains on his teeth from his licking the wound. It absolutely unnerved her. Her tone raised in pitch: "Oh… all right, th…, th…, thank you then."

There was something abrasive in his face and she was uneasy. Her stomach roiled. She was glad the job was done. She urged him toward the front door. She wanted him to leave, *now.* When Darren passed she avoided eye contact. She bit her lip. Dirt was tracked all over the carpet from his boots. Small scraps of wire were left on the carpet where he cut them and the television set was not pushed back in place. It all irritated her, got underneath her skin. But she maintained her composure. She shut the door and latched the chain as he hit the front stoop. She started to settle down. As he was closer to boarding his van and leaving, she ran her fingers through her hair, inhaled deeply, then exhaled to subdue her heavily beating heart.

Darren was across the driveway loading his van and about to disappear. She watched him, hidden behind a curtain. He removed his cap and combed his hair with his fingers, then replaced it on his head. She wanted to call the cable company and report this *Beckwith* character. Over on the kitchen island sat the phone book opened to the page she had consulted.

There it jumped out in bold print. *CABLE KING.* Her eyes studied the letters intently. *Call us at 987-The-King. Let us know how we're doing.* She visualized the crackpot who answers these types of calls, or even the "suit" that would yes her to death and do little or nothing about scum like him. He may go a step further and ask her to send a letter to headquarters somewhere on the west coast, whatever it takes to placate her without really solving the problem.

All afternoon she sat out back by the pool and caught up on her reading, relaxing, brushing off the stress, letting go of the thoughts that poisoned her mind. Her lawn chair was reclined. Magazines were strewn at the edge of the pool. A half-eaten plate of food sat next to her on a patio table. Her wine glass was empty, the bottle had a few drops left inside. A small radio was plugged in by the barbecue, the easy listening station purring the classics.

Hours later it began to drizzle, forcing her inside. After dark she chilled in her bedroom, watching an old black and white movie from the *Classics Collection* her husband gave her on her birthday. It had been raining steady for hours and intensified as the night wore on. She cranked up the volume to hear the movie over the din of spearing rain.

The lights were out in the room except for a lamp on the end table with its shadow licking the wall. It was now part of the flick she enjoyed most. She tugged the blankets under her chin and sunk her head into a thick marshmallow of pillows. Her eyes lids were heavy. Thunder rumbled outside. Faint flashes of lightning teased the moonlit sky. She watched another thirty minutes of the film and her breathing slowed, her body lulled itself to sleep. The elements were just right, conducive to napping. Her tight grip on the remote control loosened and it crashed to the floor but failed to wake her. The thunder continued its percussion, one rumble after another. She sank into unconsciousness for an hour or so. Each breath her lungs took was deep and strong, peaceful. All the doors were closed, locked, secure. Only the bedroom door was ajar. The phone was next to her in case her husband called to check in.

The storm erupted, a bolt of lightning exploded across the eerie sky. The yard lit up like a stadium. The growling thunderstorm stole her from slumber. She sat up and leaned against the headboard, wiped her face. She glanced at the clock. 11:30 P.M. Out of the blue she realized a few things had been left outside. She was glad to be awake after all. The radio, the food, the glass, magazines; the items were certainly drenched and the food attracting bugs of some kind. She hated bugs. They were everywhere. They scared her senseless. She cringed at the sight of spiders, worms, cockroaches and maggots; all of them nasty, gross, in her eyes. If she thought about the creepy-crawlies anymore she would be up all night staring around the room, paranoid.

She grabbed a raincoat from the closet and jumped into a pair of sneakers. She wore the raincoat over her pajamas. It would only take a few minutes and afterwards a shower and some rest were in order. She wanted to be ready for her family tomorrow. She went downstairs, switched on the exterior light, and stepped out onto the dimly lit deck. The lower section, the lawn in particular, was too dark, and she was unable to see much of anything.

She jumped back and screamed. Panic locked her up. The heavy rain jabbed her face. Darren Beckwith was climbing the stairs. He crossed over the threshold of darkness from the stairs and broke into the faint light on deck like a man possessed. He was dressed as before. His uniform was now pasted to his body from the soaking rain. The baseball cap tilted in reverse on his head revealed dangling, sopping wet hair that concealed part of his menacing eyes and their intentions. He smiled at her with a mouth full of gruesome teeth. She scrambled back into the house and ripped the screen door closed, locked it in place.

He chased her, covering ground fast. He moved with the grace and speed of a feline despite his gargantuan size. She gripped the handle with her hand and slammed it. As soon as it closed he tore a hole through the mesh with his bare hand. His nails did the work of daggers, slashing a path with such force that he was able to grab her skinny wrist in his powerful palm. She shrieked at the touch of his slimy fingers. They wrapped around like a handcuff of wet flesh, and his long pointed fingernails ripped into her skin, drawing blood. She attempted to jerk her hand away and he squeezed harder. With the other hand she yanked the heavy door and smashed his hand between the frame and the door, breaking his grip. She trembled, turned the latch and it clicked securely. She ran to the bedroom and locked herself in, leaped over the bed and to the phone to call 911. The line was dead. Down in the living room glass shattered and a horrifying thought scraped away in her mind. The maniac was in the house.

She fired the phone down in frustration. Fright battered her, forced her to think fast on her feet or die at the hands of a freak. She opened the window and measured the drop, thirty feet or so to the lawn. She paused for a fraction of a second; she had few left before Darren burst through the door and had his way. The door was thin and it wouldn't stand for long when his six-foot-plus, two-hundred-fifty-pound, angry body jack hammered it. She leaned out the window and estimated the drop, discovered a new kind of fear. Why had she not followed her instinct to file a complaint against this nut? She was infuriated with herself, admonished herself. A lot of good it did her now. If it happened again she would make amends for the unforgivable error, a grave mistake; if she lived through the night.

Darren barreled into the door with his shoulder, he was a human ram. The initial strike separated the molding from the frame and the door cracked dead center. It weakened the foundation but he failed to achieve entry. Rage consumed him. His deep, harsh breathing was like that of a man driven, a monster. This was his calling, his place in the world. He drove into the door relentlessly and each lunge loosened it more. Five more times with his full weight still didn't grant him access. He stopped. His shoulder ached and he rubbed it with his hand, took a few more breaths and recharged, repeated the process.

He moistened his lips with his tongue, spun and faced the opposite wall. He swung his arm backward and thrust his fist forward gutting a hole in the sheetrock. His powerful hand hollowed a gap the size of a basketball. Scraps rained down on the floor, dust was airborne. The impact from his knuckles spread cracks from floor to ceiling. The violence heightened his thirst, his hunger. He submerged himself in the pain and the release. He wanted more, needed more. He stepped back a few feet and used his work boot to kick the door. The hinges parted from the jam. Pieces of the lock snapped, wood shavings sprayed across the room. She braced herself on the window sill with her fingers latched on tightly. Twenty-five feet was the balance between life and death. She cried out as her grip faltered and her body fell to the ground. Who heard her cry for help in mid-air? Not a soul.

He charged to the window and watched her writhing below. A smile cracked his lips; he savored this moment, her panic. He thrived on the sound of her screams as she clenched at her leg in pain, tossing and turning in the grass. The rain dowsed her and her life was now in an agonizing state of terror. He licked his chops again like an animal, anticipated the sensation of her skin squashed underneath his thick fingers as they coiled around her skinny neck. Maybe once she was dead he would give her what he knew she needed; what her husband never delivered. Darren chased after her, to end it all. His blood pressure shot up from the excitement of the hunt, sent him to a place beyond his wildest dreams.

She limped into the woods. The stabbing pain in her legs felt as if a long hot poker was driven into her shins and came out through the knee caps. Her injuries were extensive and the cramping was severe. She kept going. The aches, the throbbing, ratcheted up with each stride, absorbing valuable oxygen she needed to scream for help. She had to shout loud enough to be heard over the teeming rain and the air conditioners that roared in unison on the block. She saw black spots as she faded in and out of awareness. It made her view life oddly, strangely. She suddenly regretted her sequestered life, the distance between homes; seclusion from the norm of society.

It was impossible to hear the Philipses' dog bark from two houses down or the roistering kids at summer parties. It would take forever for the cops to get here, save her. It was a laid back community where the cops had no real crime to fight so they handed out tickets for not wearing seat belts. Caravans buckled down on motorists with expired inspection stickers, but where are they when homicide is on their doorstep? The police were blue-collar robots playing up to the public. Was this the dream life she asked for? Was it a bad dream, or her worst nightmare?

She glanced up at the kitchen window and saw him walking. He stopped, and directed his gaze through the glass, readjusted his cap, and surveyed his target like the wolf its prey, his eyes pulled wide and intimidating, lupine. With resolve Darren treaded the distance from the dismantled sliders to the deck stairs. When he reached the bottom of the staircase, he sped up his pursuit.

She was gimping, stumbling, dragging her leg. Waves of intense pain slowed her, made her dizzier. She was well into the pitch-black forest when she noticed a light far away, obscured behind a wall of trees that divided the development. She stabilized her hyperactive breathing by taking deeper breaths. With the meager energy reserve that remained she let out the loudest scream her lungs could generate. She shouted for help with such pressure that it made her head pound harder, pulsate with throbbing jabs. A boulder impeded her path. She leaped and swung herself over the top. Darren grabbed her by the neck and forced her flat on her back. The ground was uneven, rocky. She winced from the collision of body and stone, but fought with punches that had no real sting behind them.

He laughed sadistically, swatting her blows away like harmless flies. This would be an easy kill. Now he would get what he came for. He fired a punch and nailed her square in the jaw. The shot transported her into an alter universe filled with flashing colors. She felt no more pain, no more of anything. Darren went to work. He unbuttoned his pants and lowered them to his ankles, then tore off her raincoat and pajamas. She was vulnerable, all alone, isolated in scrub brush and utter darkness. He spread her legs to make entering her an easy task. Suddenly, a beam of light shined on the rock to his left, then it weaved to the right and engulfed the back of his head.

"Get the fuck off her!" A female voice from behind.

He rose to his feet and pivoted, stared into the cone of light and the barrel of a pistol.

"Nice and slow, you sick bastard!" she commanded.

With a flick of the pistol she urged him away from the helpless woman.

Darren pulled up his pants and moved toward her. The handgun was trained at his head, he didn't squint.   He refused to show fear of any kind.   It became a stand off he was confident of winning.   He stepped forward again and heard the lady was regaining consciousness.   Her eyelids rolled open slowly.   One hand favored her leg and she moaned as the pain returned. Darren calculated his next move. His eyeballs stormed in circles, working every angle. He had a plan set in his mind: double homicide.   He smiled.   The gun was locked on him, her arm underneath straight out with the flashlight secured in one hand, the other rested on top with the point aimed at his head. She back-pedaled six steps and never lost her focus.   Her stance was strong and sturdy, like a marksman.

His smile faded. "Make your move, make it fast, so I can add your corpse to the pile, with the others!"

He watched the silhouette of the woman in back of the piercing light. He heard the barrel pin click into position.

"You're going to rot in hell, Beckwith."

The trigger was pulled and a bullet drilled his forehead. Darren fell backwards on top of the boulder.

On the following day her mind was clear despite the sedatives and she was reunited with her family when they returned from out of town. It was still raining but her spirits were high; she survived. She had a cast on her leg and her ribs were bandaged. Walking around on crutches was a small price to pay to be alive. She learned that it was not a stranger that came to her aide, but someone who lived on her street, a special lady whom she saw only in passing occasionally.

Her name was Felicia.

Blink of an Eye

Paul loaded the Jeep with luggage and spent time alone with his thoughts. He was at a point in life where on the exterior everything was as it should be: the job was good, the company was thriving. He and his wife were on their way to the third vacation of the year. He relished week-long getaways out of the country far away from home where nothing reminded him of the daily grind. This time they were heading to Vreeland. Renee jumped at the chance to spend quality time in the car with Paul on a road trip as opposed to hopping on a plane with hundreds of passengers. She wanted a change of pace and Paul was happy to accommodate. He strapped the bicycles in place on the rack and waited for Renee to emerge from the house. Paul glanced at his watch; the one she bought him with the built-in compass and temperature gauge.

"Damn, how much longer can she chatter? She'll see her friend next week for Christ's sake!" He stood, incredulous.

The afternoon boasted a rich blue sky. The strong sun was blazing through the windshield so he cranked the air conditioner to cool the interior. In the front pocket of his cargo shorts he had two thousand dollars in vacation money. He reached in to double check it was there and squeezed the thick fold of cash.

Renee finally glided through the doorway. Her long bleached-blonde hair drifted gently in the cool summer breeze. She never wore a stitch of make-up. He watched her gracefully stride on the long walk to the car, admiring her long legs and captivating blue eyes. The way she worked it made him want her now in the back seat, like their first time when the night ended in his Camaro out on the crest of Rackfort Cliffs. Following hours of passionate love-making they exchanged gazes. Drenched in sweat; cuddled under a warm blanket on a cold evening upon an array of sparkling stars that Renee pointed at and asked, "Which one is ours?" His head was kinked against the car door at a cumbersome angle. He replied. "All of them." Renee's watery eyes brought her angelic face to life that night.

But marriage also can unveil turbulent times and that was a lesson Paul had learned again yesterday. He was no virgin to the sadistic game of marital pitfalls. It came out of nowhere last night.

They hit a bump in the road that ended in a nasty fight. She ended up bawling her eyes out for hours and sequestered herself in the den, remaining there until this morning without an utterance. He didn't understand why she was so pissed. He had screwed up and made the mistake of defending his actions. It turned out being a debacle of huge proportions and dampened the start of their vacation. This one was the last of the year for them and Paul had reminded her days ago that upon their return it would be all work and little fun all the way to the end of winter.

Some time during last night's departure checklist Renee lost her head over pettiness. "How could you forget to put the mail on hold? I reminded you *at least* half a dozen times!" Paul pulled off his glasses and wiped his tired eyes. "Give me a break, huh!"

She stormed out of the room, evidently disgusted by his reactions as her eyes started to puddle with stress induced tears. "You never listen to me," she mumbled under her breath as she disappeared behind the living room wall. "All I ask is one simple thing, just one!"

Renee's tirade went on for a good thirty minutes, and even after he left her alone she carried on spewing more garbage he had to ignore. Better to let it blow over until she's ready to discuss it rationally, he guessed.

When she approached the Jeep she reached for the car door and decided to push his buttons, her way of unleashing her pent up aggravation from last night.

She gestured with her hand at the spare bike tire. "What's with that?" she asked, her inquiry drenched in sarcasm.

Paul bit his lip. "It's just a spare, babe. There are a ton of great trails up there, can't hurt to have an extra. Want me to show you how this rack loads and unloads?" She looked away and opened the car door, uninterested. Renee inventoried the cab. A bottle of water, a map, and a pack of gum sat in the center console. Paul entered and plopped down onto the seat.

"It's good to know you pack the incidentals," she said as her finger hovered over the items. Paul sighed; he rolled his eyes trying to dissolve her attempts to rile him up. "I plan on driving straight through, slept good last night. Just sit back and relax, okay?" Renee shot him a look, one that meant *everything* was fine and she was slowly coming back to earth from last night's feud.

The interstate was crowded. Cars were flying past them while Paul was doing a heavy-footed seventy-five. The windows were down and his shoulder length dark hair was blowing in the wind. "Vreeland looks amazing!" Renee remarked while perusing the brochures. "This place is supposed to be a vacation paradise, from what I see here it's going to be a blast."

He turned toward her and their eyes met for a brief moment. His lips bloomed into a smile and she returned his glance. Paul flipped on the radio and landed on an alternative station, kicked back into driving mode. Renee got caught up in the moment; she reached out and rested her hand on his and gently caressed it. They passed the time throwing a few jokes back and forth and recalled some of their previous vacation memories which livened up the drive. This stretch of highway flowed with steady traffic and Paul was in synch behind the wheel.

The hours passed. The sun began its descent below the horizon of tall evergreens and mountains. Paul drove a good chunk of time and the trip was unfolding as planned. Just as the map said, they encountered Interstate 75, a seemingly never-ending stretch of highway with only a few rest stops and places to eat. But it was the most efficient route to their destination and they welcomed a trip on the open road.

The journey soon turned into a long, tiresome drive as Paul squirmed in the seat and his ass was giving way to pins and needles. His legs were going numb too and the position in the car was becoming increasingly uncomfortable. He looked over at Renee, who had her head resting against the window. Her complexion was drained and pale despite her earlier enthusiasm. Perhaps she hadn't fully recovered from last night's tantrum. She hadn't said a word for over fifty miles but he maintained his focus on the situation at hand.

Paul reached behind the seat and grabbed his *Shit Happens* sweatshirt; the gag gift he bought on a cruise last year when they lost his luggage. He draped it over her. She acknowledged his consideration with a smile and then her eyes closed to rest. That was always his way of softening the mood, especially when he was unsure of what was whirling around inside her head.

The little things seemed to warm her back up, helped lift her morale, which marriage sometimes suppresses.

A few miles later he glanced into the side-view mirror and saw a car approaching on the left at a high speed. The oncoming car accelerated, and before he knew what was happening it was riding along side him on the left. Its muffler dangled from underneath and dragged the pavement, the sound was ear-piercing and sparks were flying in yellow flashes. Paul took a quick look at the driver whose eyes were plastered on him rather than the road. The strange man wore an old dirty baseball cap; a set of bushy eyebrows offset his pointy beard and dingy toothed smile. The vehicle forged ahead and then without warning, darted out in front of them, forcing Paul to swerve into the right hand lane. He used evasive action to avoid a collision as a big work truck was passing while Paul was in transit. His Jeep crossed over the entire lane and the grated shoulder, sending the car into spasm and then out of control, leaving Paul only one choice; to pull strong to the left or risk damage to the Jeep or to them. The commotion ripped Renee from the beginnings of a nap and the car, for what seemed like an eternity, was beyond Paul's control. She clutched her chest and instinctively braced herself on the dashboard with both hands.

"Paul!" She screamed in his ear as if somehow this was his fault, assuming his attention was faltering. He could tell she was thinking: *this wouldn't be the first time*, while staring him down and holding onto the vinyl dash.

He shouted back, "Calm down!" His outburst

forced Renee to retreat. "Hold on tight!" he commanded with a face wrinkled in nervousness and anger. Eventually he was able to maintain control of the vehicle and catch his breath. The suspicious car sped up and took a comfortable lead that provided a good ten car lengths between them.

"Damn it! Fucking asshole! What the hell is his problem?" he yelled.

As soon as Renee absorbed the situation she understood that Paul was up against the recklessness of some crazy driver, and one with a car that was falling apart. She saw the shoddy car weaving ahead, the muffler scraping the ground setting off a cluster of flashes below. Paul let out this deep angry groan and trails of tension spread on his forehead. Renee saw the anger brewing inside him. His face was flustered and twice he pounded the steering wheel with his right fist. Paul slammed on the gas. The motor whined in high gear. She didn't like the way the situation was unfolding, so she grabbed a handful of his shirt sleeve and yanked it hard. "What the heck are you doing? Let it go!"

He trembled violently. "Sorry, I have to get this out or—"

She raked her hands through her hair in a nervous frenzy. "Please, leave this alone."

Paul caught up to the car. They were a couple car lengths away. Sparks were still flying from the destroyed muffler and Paul, pushing his Jeep harder, was gaining ground on the passenger side. Renee sat tight with her face in her palms, terrified of the situation. He was now side by side with the car and the driver wouldn't even look at him. Again, Renee tugged at his shirt and he pulled away from her grasp. "Fuck you, man!" he shouted to the crazy driver, giving him the finger. When he was through venting he pinned the accelerator and found a stretch of open road to get far away from the whack job, then the two of them could finally take the edge off and settle down.

He took a swig of the bottled water and passed it over to Renee who nodded *no thank you.* He finally came down from his fit of rage and regained his sense of responsibility. She was a little tensed up in her seat with her knees curled into her chest. He leaned toward her, stroked her cheek with his hand and a smile began to appear on his face.

"Sorry about that," he said in a somber tone.

Renee understood the unusual circumstances he had to overcome. "It wasn't your fault. We're okay now. I'm going to get some shut eye. I feel a little out of it."

Paul winked. "You go ahead, I got it from here. You relax."

The hours steam-rolled past them, the sun was long gone. The breeze was now stronger and refreshed the warm and sticky August evening. The moon was cut in half and any sign of stars was hidden behind a cloak of cloud cover. He had covered hundreds of miles and hung in there despite the day's hurdles. His weary mind started to drift and to stay awake he reminisced about his college days, the long excursions that kept him awake all night behind the wheel when he visited friends on long weekend hang-outs in Vermont and up North. Here he was yawning non-stop for the last hour. He refused to disturb Renee. She was sound asleep in the seat, reclined and wrapped up in his sweatshirt. Her hair flowed over the cushion and almost touched the floor. When he glanced in her direction he felt his heart twitch; she looked so precious, so peaceful.

Another hour flew past and the road became desolate and void of traffic. Occasionally an eighteen-wheeler or motorcycle would pass. Nothing but dark highway as far as his headlights could shine. Fatigue intensified and tested his ability to focus. At least twice in the last five miles he felt his head rolling forward and his eyes wanting to seal. He tried to look alive and keep his attentiveness, hell-bent on getting to their destination and starting off the vacation fresh. He popped a piece of chewing gum in his mouth thinking it would help him stay alert; sharpen the senses, keep the juices flowing. Ahead a sign came into view. The reflective letters indicated a list of cities. Paul was happy to see some sign; some proof that they were getting closer. They hadn't encountered anything for what seemed like forever. They approached the sign that was partially obscured with pine tree branches, the letters leaped at him in the cone of the headlights.

Belstar- 25 miles

Krickstown- 50 miles

Vreeland- 150 miles

The sign awarded him a second wind, a new lease on his energy; a reason to keep going. He stuck his head out the window and inhaled a deep rush of clean air, then shifted into high gear and pressed on. He was set on going the distance now, just like his glory days when he was a weekend warrior. The whole time he was glad Renee was asleep. How wonderful the moment will be when she wakes up and he's checking them into a comfortable romantic getaway. He embarked on this phase of the trip with pure adrenaline. She was snoring softly along side him. He locked in and sped up. There hadn't been a sign of police anywhere so he let his lead foot do the driving.

It was late, thirty miles later, and Paul had the interstate to himself. He had one problem though; one small roadblock. He was wearing down again and that sweet rush that consumed him earlier had pushed aside— exhaustion was working its way in. His energy was dwindling with each mile and it would be impossible to make it to Vreeland without rest. He had to accept that emotional hardship. It was that simple. He couldn't forge ahead without a break. He couldn't bear to wake Renee and ask her to take the wheel. That was an idea he refused to consider. They had seen no rest stops or hotels on this road. Way back about thirty miles ago they crossed a bridge where a gas station sign stood tall over the exit ramp, but stubbornness prevented him from stopping.

He imagined the necessary jolt one cup of coffee would bring him if he could only find someplace to stop off. He pushed himself a few more miles and it made the situation much worse. His eye lids were heavy and cracking down and he was losing the desperate battle to keep himself alert. The road in front of him became distorted from his declining concentration. A horrible feeling consumed him. What if he fell asleep at the wheel and something happened to Renee? He couldn't live with that. He dared not risk her life or his own just to go a little farther. The longer he pressed on the greater the probability of danger, a risk he wasn't prepared to take. In the center console his eyes met up with the water bottle. He swallowed a mouthful of water and splashed some on his face to dispel the sluggishness. It was useless. He had to think of an alternative. The trip had become an uphill battle he was quickly losing. He used the only option he had and it was the safest solution to the problem.

Paul pulled the Jeep to the side of the road. He took a deep breath and adjusted the seat away from the wheel to free up his legs. The Jeep was wedged in between a row of tall trees in a woody alcove out of direct sight of the interstate. Passing vehicles or a cop would be unable spot him. Paul looked around at the surroundings. The woods were dark and quiet, but this is what he had to do. He peeked at Renee. She was sound asleep in the seat and had been for hours. His watch alarm was a convenience he took advantage of. He set it to go off in thirty minutes. That would be enough time to close his eyes and gather the steam for the next round at the wheel and bring them in. He hit the button and the power locks clicked into place. The windows were closed most of the way, the interior was comfortable and cool. With his index finger he pushed the switch, reclined the seat into position, and gave in to the urge—closed his eyes. For a brief moment he enjoyed that simple feeling of resting his heavy lids and then before he knew what was happening, he fell asleep.

The moon poked through eerie sky and shifted its glow over the woods and onto the Jeep. Renee tossed and turned in her seat and she started to stir. A *clicking* sound made her head twitch, her eyeballs rolled oddly behind her lids. She turned over and faced the passenger side door. Only a few cars passed while she soundly rested and not one of them saw their hide-out. Out of the blue the car jerked. Renee's eyes popped open to darkness with a splash of moonlight on the dashboard. It took her a second or two to get her bearings. With the sweatshirt sleeve she wiped away the cobwebs from the corner of her eyes and then turned to the left. Paul was gone. She looked out every window for a sign of him; there was nothing. She pulled the hair back from her face. "Paul?" she called out, and paused a second waiting for him to respond, continued to scout the perimeter. He was likely taking a leak or stretching his legs, she guessed. "Paul?"

The second calling brought no response. Renee hit the button to lower the window, it didn't budge. The keys were gone from the ignition and immediately she knew something was terribly wrong. Suddenly her heart misfired, the pit of her stomach felt deep and hollow. On the console were the empty bottle of water and the pack of gum. She opened the door and yelled. "PAUL, PAUL! ARE YOU OUT

THERE?"

Utter silence chilled her to the bone. Her lips trembled; her shaking hands rose to her mouth. For the first time in their life together Paul was not at her side. He was always there when she needed him. Even on the days when their marriage seemed hopelessly bogged down and they felt they were at a crossroads, he was there.

A branch snapped. Something moved out there in the pitch-black depths. It was impossible to see ahead and into the thicket of trees and brush. It was too dark and she needed a flashlight to map out a path. She got out of the car and kept glued to the body of the Jeep until she arrived at the hatch. She popped the latch, rummaged through the storage, and stumbled upon a flashlight. Renee pushed the rubber nipple and the flashlight fired to life with a strong bright beam.

Leaves crackled in the dark sprawl of the forest and the crunch hooked her attention as she steered the light into the woods. She waved it everywhere, at ground level first, then into the trees, and then landed the lamp deep into the scrub brush. Her body began to shiver, and although it was a warm night, the fear and isolation tunneled through her, rendering her flesh ice cold. She had trouble departing from the car. She stood five feet from the driver's side door, closed her eyes, remembering Paul's soft and reassuring hand caressing her face. Her eyes bulged with tears. Little streams of despair rolled down her face as she dropped to her knees and wept. Her gut-wrenching session ended, for now. She knew it was important to search for help and for her husband. Staying at the car was a death sentence.

She tried to unlatch the bike from the rack but the darkness and her failure to listen to Paul's instructions earlier proved to be a crushing blow. Renee fiddled with the device and as she did more weird noises stalked the night. She was getting nowhere and growing increasingly frightened, and slowly losing control of the situation. Renee weaved through the brush, stepping over cumbersome tree roots and prickly vegetation. After covering a quick thirty feet she came onto the interstate and followed the narrow shoulder. All kinds of horrid scenarios ran amok in her mind. Where was Paul? Was he alive? Did he walk out on her without warning? These depressing snapshots played tricks with her mind. She started hearing strange noises all around her; things going bump in the night, snapping branches and shifting leaves. Every sound she heard only became more unbearable as she trudged alone in the dark in the middle of nowhere.

Ahead was just a long winding street without a sign of life. Renee walked another thirty minutes and her flashlight reflected off a mile marker. It stood ten feet in front of her, and the closer she came the slower she moved until her progress was stopped dead in its tracks. The white florescent sign was spackled with blood. Her imagination went into overdrive. She felt her intestines twist into knots. Her legs and feet worked independently, drawing her closer to the marker. Her flashlight shined on a devastating discovery. It was certainly human blood splattered all over the street sign. Thick blood, deep red, drizzled from the top, coating the number 2, and trickling down over a 6 and then a 1.

Renee stood erect, quivering like it was the middle of winter and she was nude in the elements. The tears flowed again and mixed with her summer sweat. It had to be Paul's blood. Somebody had known she'd find the evidence soon enough. Her arms and legs wobbled at the thought of how the stains got there. What was done to him? Was he suffering somewhere? Why was *she* left unharmed? She scoped the surroundings, wanting desperately to find a path or a clue. Renee threw the light in every direction, even to the sky in desperation, knowing overhead was nothing but a haunting sky and no one to help her. She had to pull herself together. Paul was out there. Renee drew an imaginary line in her head from the mile marker straight back into the woods with her beam. She would commit to that much. Not a car had passed by since she left hers and now the mission was to find Paul, even if it meant paying with her life. Once more she walked ahead, hugging the narrow shoulder.

Renee jumped back and dropped her flashlight. The light fizzled and she was engulfed in total darkness. It was Paul's wristwatch, abandoned ten feet ahead of the marker. Her horrific thoughts, the frightening visions; they were now culminating into a reality she wanted no part of, and the powerful force rattled her nervous system to its core. Renee screamed at the top of her lungs. "PAUL! PAUL!" The words flew out from her dry throat in painful bursts. "Where are you?" she howled in terror.

Although the unknown threatened her sanity she had to keep her wits for the sake of his life and her own. She picked up the flashlight and tapped the head a few times urging it to rekindle. No such luck. Her efforts were useless. She advanced, took the wristwatch in her hand, and slid her fingers across the sprinkles of blood on the band. She had enough light to see the compass but any attempt to use it would have proved fruitless. She had no sense of direction. All the times when Paul tried to demonstrate its function, she ignored his little lessons and kept flipping through her magazines, paying no attention to the things he wanted to teach her. What she wouldn't give now to immerse herself into such a mundane conversation. Maybe snuggle up next to him on the couch while he played with his toy like a little kid and kissed her, thanking her for the gift.

Renee spun in circles to search for a light of some kind. Her eyes had adjusted to the darkness well enough to see the long stretch of highway ahead and behind her; not so much as a streetlamp was burning near of far. Dense woods surrounded her with a terror, whether it was monster or human she did not know, but it was waiting in the wings, dwelling in a thick shield of black, watching her. She considered returning to the car but without keys there was no point. She was no more protected there than she was here. Her body was tired and drained and she had ventured far. She contemplated her next move. The only sensible thing to do was follow the clue she had in her hand and plunge deeper into threatening chaos for a sign of Paul. She couldn't continue, not knowing what happened to him. She believed he was alive and that was all she needed to enter the woods.

Renee entered the first section and tangles of vines and thorny brush clawed at her lower body. As she walked deeper it was as though the forest came to life and groped her flesh. Something mushy rubbed against her cheek and left a slimy residue. She brought her hand up to feel what it was and her fingertips came away covered with a chunky substance. She took a whiff and the fetid odor repulsed her. It had the texture of gelatin and the odor was akin to fecal matter. She ran ahead and met up with a tree that she braced herself against, waiting for a bout of nausea to pass. Renee was beyond disoriented but felt her way around with her hands and outstretched arms. Her steps became slower and more deliberate as she probed further into the inhospitable dungeon of her worst fears. She heard a noise; then the sound came toward her quickly. Twigs snapped and split within earshot. Her eyes tracked the noise. There, standing before her, wrapped in the darkness, she saw an enormous thing.

A man? A monster? Renee had no idea what the hell it was and it didn't matter. She was petrified. The form emitted an abnormal sound, something she had never heard before; a deep and phlegm-laden groan that made her shake and panic. Her body felt like it was weighted down and the walls of doom were closing in fast around her. The attempt to talk or scream was impossible. Her throat was coarse and dry and the figure didn't move. She could hear it breathe, smell its repulsive odor, see its form take shape as her eyes focused intently in the dark with a slim drizzle of moonbeam bleeding through the canopy of pines. They were at a stand still when Renee tried to produce wispy sounds with her mouth.

"Do you—?"

No chance for her to finish. Her words were cut short by that towering figure standing ten feet from her. The thing bolted for her. Renee turned and ran desperately. She wept and the tears spilled down her face. She tasted the salty sediment creeping into her mouth. The thing's footsteps crunched in rapid bursts behind her, although she was gaining a comfortable lead. The barberry was ruthlessly slicing into her arms and legs. Her feet twisted and slipped over the endless obstacle course of woody and rocky terrain. The charging figure took short, shallow breaths and whatever it was broke its silence with two words.

"Your turn!"

It sounded like some nefarious cry, almost as if the voice was antagonizing from underwater. Renee had no idea what it meant, or who it was. She crossed the last row of bramble and made it to the street. Her stamina was surprisingly holding strong. She ran hard and sustained her pace, no longer hearing the marathon breathing or the haunting echo of the dark figure that was behind her. She felt trails of blood worming down her arms and legs. But down the road in front of her was the most wonderful thing she had seen all night.

A set of headlights was slicing a path through the night on the interstate and approaching fast. The gargling motor leased her hope for a moment as it closed the gap between them. Her tears became a fusion of sheer terror and sweet relief. Out of the blue a rock struck the back of her head. Renee plummeted to the ground face first. Her entire body slid across the graveled surface, tearing apart her delicate skin. The car skidded to a stop. An old man jumped from a station wagon and ran to Renee's aide. Without thinking for even a split second, the man rolled her over and hooked his arms underneath her armpits, pulling her toward the wagon. Luckily, he managed to get her close and dropped her onto the corner of the bench seat. The old man's heart raced feverishly and he grabbed his chest, but he didn't give up. He used his lower body and hips to thrust her all the way in and he slammed the door. He bent down to get in the car and was blindsided. His skull was bashed with Renee's flashlight. The old man dropped to the ground and was dragged toward the woods.

Renee was slowly rising out of unconsciousness and shaking off the clouds in her head. She tried to sit up and heard the struggle going on away from the car. The attacker was bludgeoning the old man to death with the flashlight. Renee heard the man pleading for his life, the *thud* of the flashlight was horrifying as it repeatedly pounded the man all over his body. With each strike she heard the man's bones crunch. His cries were filled with agony. She knew it was only a matter of time until the killer came back for her. Everything was still a blur. She was drained of the strength to flee or to muster a defense against the brutal attack that was pending. She couldn't fight the weariness that constricted her; she felt drugged. Her whole body was limp and lifeless; when the rock struck the back of her head she had collapsed and never felt the impact. New frightening thoughts consumed her. With the miniscule amount of energy she had left she thought of Paul and now she was sick with defeat. Would she never find him, never know what happened to him, even if he was still alive? Was there more she could've done?

She heard the lunatic's heavy breathing, more pronounced than before. The wagon rocked and the door slammed. Her head started pounding, thumping with fierce blows against the inside of her cranium, and the pain was too intense to stand against or ignore. Blood and road fragments distorted what little she saw as she felt them leaking from the lesions on her face; her mouth and eyes were caked with scaled flesh. As afraid as she was to fall asleep, she could not resist her body's urge to surrender. Renee came to a saddening realization. This was how it was going to end and maybe if she let go and closed her eyes, she could find Paul in another place.

Renee succumbed, and behind her eyes the world was white as a December snowfall. She saw one more thing that helped her float away and leave everything behind. It was that moment that warmed her heart as if she was sitting in front of a crisp, crackling fire. It happened when they first met and made love under the stars. Their gazes crossed paths and she asked him which star was theirs. He smiled and told her, "All of them." Now Renee understood the meaning of life, and how it can change in the *blink of an eye.*

Dead End

'm driving along, innocently, and suddenly this stranger decides to ride my ass playing some sick game. Why won't they just go around me? For miles high beams have blinded me. I've tried to ignore them and keep my eyes locked on the dark highway. I change lanes, they follow. Some lunatic has an axe to grind and they've got the wrong guy. Maniac! Just disappear, and leave me the hell alone! I did *nothing* wrong.

This is crazy— after such a wonderful time with Janine, lying in the grass, whispering sweet things in her ear. Janine, the seductress, making me feel alive again, making me feel as a real man *should* feel. All I want is to get home and get some frigging sleep, forget about the whole damn thing. That was our last time; no more, it's out of hand. I accelerate and the truck behind me closes the gap. I hear the *thud* of our bumpers colliding and my Dodge lurches forward and my neck snaps back. This stretch of Interstate 24 is creepy and empty and I feel trapped in a deadly battle of roulette. The truck is drafting me, pushing me faster, prodding. I want to see the prick but darkness shields what I'm sure will be the face of some psycho.

I try to slow down, but now I can't! I fear a collision, and that monstrous push-bar staring back at me in the mirror will tear my two-door to shreds. The situation is growing more dangerous by the second, spiraling out of control, and all I see is a truck towering over my rear. I feel like a fly caught in a spider's deadly web. The sight of long, furry legs crawling toward it, closer…closer, the fly realizing death is near, soon to be stung, paralyzed, devoured. I spin around and that monstrous steel push-bar looks like teeth about to chop and annihilate my truck, then the backseat, then *me.*

"Get off my ass you sick mother fucker!" I shout from the cab even though no one can hear me. The road is barren. Suddenly the interior of my car is flooded with more blinding light, fog lights; the set of powerful halogens fires down into my cab stealing my focus from the road ahead. There must be a lever in his truck that controls them. They slide back and forth and singe my pupils. Now staring at the windshield is like staring into the sun. I squint in pain. I adjust the rearview mirror to shield my eyes from the oppressive beams. Spots are dancing in my vision, orbs flashing. A spectrum of color flickers in my sight.

My car fishtails like an angry snake. I weave across the yellow line and then back again. The truck refuses to back off. My engine is pushed to the limit. The four-cylinder motor roars. The speedometer is twitching at eighty-five. My screaming motor is unable to transcend and I think it's going to *blow.* The front end of my car is trembling, it jerks side to side. The wheel is hard to handle and it takes on a life of its own, shimmying under my grip. An empty wine bottle is rolling around on the passenger-side floor and thrashing against the seat legs.

Clang...Clang...Clang. "Damn it! I forgot to get rid of that in the park dumpster!"

I struggle to steady the car as it swings erratically in the lane. My slithering car forces the bottle to collide with the metal seat leg harder this time, and the impact shatters it. Shards of glass litter the carpeted floor. "Shit! How do I clean that before I get home?" I arrive at a fork in the road and veer to the right. The tires are screeching. A cloud from the smoking rubber seeps through the windows. I *still* can't lose this nut! The howling truck engine carves up the night and has intensified my galloping heart beat.

Suddenly the cab of the truck comes alive from an interior light. I see a figure with a broad and imposing upper body. A shotgun is clenched in his right hand. The left is steering the truck. Who is he? I take another quick look. It's impossible to make out anything more than…What? Holy shit! He's wearing a mask. Only one thing is unmistakable; a shotgun is wrapped in his thick palm. The sick bastard points it at me. I'm going to die, I know it. A side street is up ahead and it may be my last chance to try and ditch him.

I yank the wheel to the right and make a hairpin turn. My car is out of control. I'm tilted on two wheels, almost capsize. It was the only escape I saw; the only way to free myself and get home, a few miles away. I slam on the brake and the car skids to a halt, my hands tremor at the ten and two. My eyes scroll the dark perimeter. Ahead there is a sign that reads *Dead End.*

Finally, the truck vanished. Now I struggle to calm myself. The deep breaths I swallow are useless. I am unglued, walking a fine edge. My palms are cold and clammy. I'm losing my grip on the wheel and reality altogether. My heart is racing a fierce beat in my chest. My composure has abandoned me for now and I feel so alone and frightened, the car idling. Deep, dark woodland left, right and in front of me. The truck is gone. Where did it go? Smoke from my tires drifts up over the hood of the car. My evasive actions caused a small crack to form on the windshield and each slice in the glass is elongating.

I hear a *crunch* to the left and I pivot my head in its direction. A large tree branch is flapping. Was that from a breeze or is something or someone out there watching me? Stalking me? I slam on the gas and make a break for it. My heart is still jack-hammering. I'm driving, shivering, completely freaked out and anxious to lock myself in my home and seal all the windows and doors, tell Karen and the kids about this and then call the police. God forbid something was to happen to them!

I make it home and sprint to the front entrance. I enter the house and burst through my bedroom door, shouting for Karen at the top of my lungs.

"Karen! Karen!"

She's not here. She's nowhere in sight. Please! Oh no! Please! Not her! Not them! Suddenly a piece of paper jumps out at me off the dark blue pillow at the head of our bed. My mind is racing. My body is a jumble of nerves, on the verge of ruin. I fear the worst. Is someone after us? Did they get to my wife and kids first? Are they hurt? Are they alive? Are they dead somewhere? I approach the paper with slow, heavy steps. I lumber toward the bed ridden with dread and filled with unbridled fear, afraid of what I will find written in ink.

The note is definitely Karen's handwriting. I hold it up to my face and bright red scribble springs up at me off the white background.

Warning!

If you cheat on me again scumbag, I'll have him finish what he started. You're alive for the sake of our children. I hope that I've made myself clear. I'm at a friend's with the kids. Now that I have your attention, think long and hard about what you did to this family because eyes are upon you. You just try and test me again you unfaithful piece of shit.

We'll be in touch………………………….Karen

Deadly Secret

It had been raining for hours and it wasn't forecasted to let up until morning. Mike drove carelessly, exceeding the speed limit in route to Nathan Callahan's party across town. He'd been drinking quite a few before he bolted from his college friend's house, leaving his date behind with her crowd and his sister. But he had promised his pal Nathan that he would stop by his bash, which was thrown together last minute over in Bostwick Township. Mike was a good man. When he gave his word he stuck to it, no matter what the circumstances, and he had promised to visit his buddy at some point tonight. His girlfriend Sandy was having a blast with his sister Melanie, and although he was enjoying himself there Mike remembered his earlier promise. "Look San, you stick around here with my sis and I'll just shoot over, make an appearance, and be back here in a flash."

Sandy reached up and gave him a kiss on the lips. "Be careful. It's pouring out there and Nathan's on the other side of Bostwick, and this time of night Route 79's a ghost highway."

Mike ran his hand through her long, silky black hair and kissed her forehead. "You worry too much," he said, pulling her close. "See you later."

Mike was cruising along 79. His wiper blades worked tirelessly on the windshield, pushing away the spearing rain. He flicked on the radio and the local station was playing a string of 80's rock classics. Mike drummed on his lap with the right hand and steered with the left. The highway was quiet, just as

Sandy told him it would be. The tops of the hemlock and pine trees were swaying in the coarse, relentless wind. Aside from the inclement weather it was the perfect time to travel this highway. The police rarely patrolled the strip this late at night and he could be a little heavier on the pedal. Mike kept a comfortable pace for a good ten miles, keeping locked in around fifty. A little fast for the conditions but he was also a little anxious to see his friend Nathan. He reached into the glove compartment for a pack of smokes that he remembered Sandy leaving there in the afternoon. As his arm extended across the dashboard it put him off balance and the car jerked. That was all it took to have him abort the idea of a smoke altogether. He straightened up and kept his focus on the dark, blurry road ahead. He didn't have much farther to go and soon he would hit Tanner Road and that would place him right in the center of Bostwick Township where Nathan resided.

He started to slow his pace to compensate for the throttling rain that thudded the windshield glass. A few miles down the road the car hesitated and a strange disturbance forced his attention to the dashboard gauges. A bright yellow blip shined behind the steering column.

"Shit!" Mike spit out in frustration. The fuel light was pulsating behind the glass veneer of the dash. He reached into the pocket of his denim jacket and realized he was without his wallet. He slapped the steering wheel to vent his stupidity and then began checking his pockets. The front seat was organized and clean, not so much as a wrapper littered the cab. The wallet wasn't in his possession, or in the car. He was screwed. Sandy had his wallet in her purse. He handed it to her when she asked for money to run into a convenience store on the Boulevard before the party. His mind raced while he forged a way out of his untimely predicament.

He stayed on track. The dreary night soon became less disastrous and more hospitable. There ahead, partially concealed in a cluster of pines, was this huge florescent sign with symbols for a gas station and a phone. He let out a sigh of relief and pulled quickly to the shoulder. The rain intensified again, battering the hood with a reckless fury. The drops bounced off the metal and rivers of water cascaded off the sides of the hood in heavy streams. Mike hit the button to ignite his emergency flashers and popped off the seat belt. Frantically, he performed a thorough search of his jeans, his jacket, and the door pockets again. Then, miraculously, he recalled that he planned ahead for an episode like this when he concealed a back up gas card inside the passenger-side visor a few months ago. He pulled down the cloth visor and there it was, just as his memory served. "Yes!" he shouted.

He buckled up and drove along Route 79 another half mile and encountered the exit sign staring back at him a few hundred feet ahead. He flipped on the right directional and veered off the ramp onto a straightaway. The unrelenting gas gauge cautioned again, *Beep-Beep-Beep.* The yellow warning light changed into a crimson glow and the letters winked incessantly from behind the dash plate. *Warning-Fuel-*

Warning-Fuel-Warning-Fuel. The caution message didn't worry Mike now. He pulled into the gas station and rolled up to the pumps. A huge sign hung over the front office window.

Marty's Self-Service

Gasoline-Diesel-Repairs-Inspections

Open for gas 24 Hours.

Restrooms- an arrow pointing down the side of the office on the west end of the building.

Mike got out of the car and hustled toward the office, holding his hands out to shield his face from the rain. He brushed into the door and it slowly closed. *Bing-Bing-Bing*, a bell chirped behind him as it swung against the glass like a pendulum. Whoever was in charge seemed to be taking their time getting to the front desk. The station interior was ordinary but neat. Belts hung from hooks. Boxes with filters and small parts were stacked orderly on the shelves behind the desk, and the right side wall was piled high with new batteries still in boxes. A man finally emerged from the back storage area. He wore brown coveralls with a patch sewn onto the left chest. The name *Dalton* was scripted across the fabric. A greasy rag was overflowing from his front waist pocket. His long hair was wrapped in a pony tail and his clean shaven face was accented with a tuft of hair dangling from his chin. Mike handed him the gas card. "Fill up on Pump #2 please." The attendant stared at the card and grinned, scratching at the back of his head.

"Sorry man, but…" He pointed at the wall. There was a list of accepted credit cards and Mike's wasn't any good there.

"Can't use this one here, just those," pointing at the display. "Or cash. What'll it be, Mister?"

Mike leaned back from the counter and he looked at the floor in disappointment. "Look, dude. I'm on my way across town to a friend's and my fuel gauge is harassing me. She's running on fumes. My girlfriend's got my friggin' wallet. Cut me a break, all right."

The attendant reached across the long counter to a stack of blank invoices with the Marty's logo printed on them. Mike grew antsy and turned back towards the door. A wave of rain thrust into the windows and rattled the door, setting off the entrance chime again. The rain was so strong he could hardly see his car through the distorted glass. It hadn't tapered off even the slightest.

"What's your name, friend?" the attendant asked. Mike glanced at him, puzzled. "Why?" he questioned rudely.

The attendant placed an empty invoice sheet in front of him and pulled a pen from his chest pocket, plopping it down next to the form. "Write your name, address, and phone number here and it'll be our own little *IOU.* You look straight up to me. He'll send you a bill. Marty is a reasonable guy."

Mike began filling out the form. He was in no mood to negotiate. The sooner he got back on the road the quicker this whole ordeal would be over with. Then the beers started boxing in his bladder. When he completed filling it out the attendant tapped the clean paper with his dirty finger. "License plate too, sir."

Mike's feet shuffled on the floor. "Can I use the bathroom back there? I need to take a piss real bad."

The man tucked the form under the metal clipboard and draped it over a hook attached to a pegboard wall behind him. A row of clipboards hung next to it with pending repairs. "Be my guest, door's open."

He ran from the office to the bathroom with his jacket canopied over his head. He rounded the corner and opened the bathroom door. The pungent odor of urine and feces leached up his nostrils. He flinched from the stink. The men's room was a disaster. The mirror was cracked. A roll of toilet paper was unrolled on the floor in a heap. The lone stall door was dangling from the hinge and the toilet was overflowing with human excrement. Graffiti covered the cinderblock walls and a used condom sat on the soap ledge.

An exhaust fan hung over the grungy toilet, and below in red paint was written: *The smell of death lingers here.*

Mike hurried to finish urinating but then something odd and mysterious caught his attention. To his right, the wind whistled through a hole about the size of a silver dollar, and the surging draft chilled his skin. He couldn't void his bladder fast enough. He tried to speed things up but the beers wreaked havoc on him. Curiously, he peeked through the hole in the cement and saw an old van parked across the lot with the double doors facing him. A motion light above the dumpster lit and faded with the blowing wind. Mike noticed a red streak on the right hand door. *Is that blood?* he wondered dreadfully.

Suddenly, the right-hand door creaked open and Mike swallowed. The next breath was lost in his dry throat. An arm flopped out from the gap between the two doors and fell over the bumper. He finally finished urinating and left the restroom. But he had to know more.

Outside was a different story. Mike wanted to walk away and forget about what he had discovered through that peephole. But he knew what he saw was real and worth investigating; tangible and terrifying. Sheer morbid curiosity tugged him closer to the van and he advanced with consternation swelling inside him. This was something he had to see, and then he'd flee this place and never return again.

Back to back rumbles of thunder growled and a series of lighting bolts split the sky into pieces. As he inched closer the rain saturated him and the clothes hung from his body like wet rags. He kept wiping the rain from his eyes but his vision blurred again in an instant.

Mike was six feet from the van and what he saw from a hole in the filthy bathroom was confirmed. He uncovered a horror more repulsive than the squalid bathroom he left moments ago. A woman's arm dangled from the van. A diamond ring was on her finger and her veins were sliced open. Blood trailed down the forearm and over the fingers. His eyes opened wide, darted back and forth, and then rolled in circles of disjointed terror. He choked as the storm's fury angled the rainwater into his mouth. Mike's eyes snaked deeper into the van as far as they could go. He saw the stack of bodies layered up to the roof. The windows were stained and streaked with blood and the odor of death stole his breath away.

Out of the blue the lights went out in the gas station behind him and the motion light faded out atop the dumpster. He was engulfed in darkness. A voice spoke to him. The words traveled through the dark in deep monotone. "You couldn't mind you business, could you?"

"Who the *fuck*?" Mike spun around, frightened.

A pause. The men stood opposing each other

at considerable distance, maybe twenty-five feet. The attendant started walking to Mike's left, and in doing so set off the sensor which rekindled the motion light.

"I want my victims to suffer internally first. I enjoy watching fear devour their soul; consume their thoughts, like a school of maggots were unleashed in their head. That kind of gnawing is what you're going to feel. You seem like a guy who keeps his *MOUTH SHUT.* It's time for your test."

Mike was shaken. He frantically searched for an escape route while shifting to the right away from the van.

"Before you get any ideas, I'll warn you only once… say a word about this to anyone and I'll kill that brunette of yours. That's a nice picture of her hanging from the mirror. What a precious thing to lose, Mike. I'll waste her and then skull-fuck her cold corpse when I'm done."

Mike felt his heart shrivel up. He imagined this man's hands around Sandy's neck, squeezing her to death or some other depraved method of torture. His eyes swayed toward the pumps where his car was and he saw the ground he had to cover for an escape. If he ran like hell he believed it possible to outrun the attendant and get to his car. Lucky for him, the maniac kept moving to his left and that opened more room on the right; breathing room when the moment struck. Mike knew to choose his moment of escape wisely. He'd get one chance. Any mistake would put him in the van with the rest of the dead bodies. He continued sliding along as the man inched closer, and then suddenly he heard a knife being pulled from a sheath.

Mike made a break for it. He ran hard. The waterlogged clothing weighed him down but it didn't affect his frantic scramble for his life. With each stride he felt his soaking wet socks sloshing in his sneakers. He slowed as he approached the car but lost his footing and stumbled onto the hood, colliding with the fringe of the quarter panel. He shouted in pain and fell to the ground. A laceration opened on his upper lip and blood slid over his mouth and down his chin. He looked back quickly and the crazed attendant hadn't emerged from the darkness yet.

He recovered, clumsily got into the car, and fired up the ignition. The car roared to life and Mike looked up. The man stood with a six-inch blade gripped between his teeth. A nearby light post fired aglow and illuminated his sadistic gesture. With his index finger the attendant tapped his temple as if to say, *remember,* and then inserted the dagger into his mouth as far as it could go until the handle alone jutted out from his mouth. Mike's eyes sprawled open and his wet face broke into spasm.

He sped away. He pinned the accelerator and blazed through the rain. Even with the wipers swinging full power, visibility was poor. He battled to keep the car in line but on the turns the car slipped on the slick surface and kicked out. Mike made another startling discovery. The gas alert was no longer flashing. He had not been near the car since he entered the station. The lunatic must've done it. *That's how he saw Sandy's photo. He searched the car when*

I was in the bathroom and had taken the god damn thing. These were the thoughts drilling through his head.

He crossed over into Bostwick and arrived at his friend's party. Inside, the place was swarming with guests and it was difficult to move. Mike weaved through the mass of people and came to the kitchen where Nathan stood, smoking pot. Mike approached his friend and they shook hands, although Nathan was stoned out of his mind. "You're nuts, Nath…I told you I'd stop by and see what's up."

Nathan was wobbling on his legs and swaying in the kitchen doorway. Mike was disappointed in him. Sure it was his party, but the long trek over to see his friend was pointless. Nathan was out of it. He was talking incoherently and struggling to stay on his feet.

Mike tried to steal a moment with Nathan to discuss what just happened. His friend was in no condition for small talk, completely oblivious to his alarm.

Mike heard a ruckus from the living room. It was the partygoers shouting. Many of them were pointing outside and laughing as bright red lights danced across the large bay window. A knock at the door. A minute passed and no one answered it. The doorbell rang. *Ding-Dong-Ding-Dong-Ding-Dong,* it chimed in a rapid-fire sequence. The sound soared throughout the living room. One of the partiers lowered the music and everybody fell silent.

A young man with a girl glued to his arm answered the door and two policemen came into the house walking like they had a board in their asses. Mike was relieved to see the gleaming badges close up in the foyer. The overhead chandelier provided sheen to their polished steel tags. The officers were armed with service revolvers, and a club dangled from a metal clip on their belts. One officer, who was easily six feet, two-hundred pounds, had a long steel flashlight clutched in his thick palm. Wings of tension fluttered inside of Mike. His head scrambled with the dilemma of *Tell? Don't tell?* He walked around the couch in front of him and slowly approached the officers.

The room froze in his mind. He was close enough to read the names on the badges. The tallest guy was *Montoya,* a tough-looking Spanish guy who appeared to be made of iron. His biceps stretched his shirt sleeve and he was intimidating to look at with his square jaw and moustache. His partner was shorter, five-eight or so but no less imposing. The name *Winewski* stood out on his shiny badge. He listened to Montoya give the group a warning. "If I get called back here again, I cuff and take names. Got it?"

What he saw in the gas station was on the tip of his tongue. He sidestepped playing the deadly game. The urge to reveal every horrifying detail was hard to resist. The words scratched and clawed for release. He shook Winewski's hand and asked "Busy night?"

The cop responded with a mellow, commanding tone. "Quiet, until now. Somebody called this disturbance in ten minutes ago. So knock it off. Keep it down."

Mike took no chances. What if the maniac found out somehow, someway? It's not worth the risk of endangering Sandy. He let the opportunity slip away.

It was after midnight when Mike returned to see Sandy and Melanie again. "What the heck took you so long?" Sandy asked.

Mike fought back tears. His eyes welled up and he pulled her in and hugged her strong. "Are you all right, Mike? You're shaking. Your lip's fat and bleeding. You're soaked to the bone! What happened?"

Mike looked at the floor and Melanie passed him a towel to dry off. He wiped his face and neck and tears leaked from the corners of his eyes. "A frustrating night is all. Flat tire, bumped my head changing it. I ran out of gas too. Ah…"

Sandy rubbed his arm and concern paled through her complexion. Her cheeks burned alive, fiery red. "At least you're here, and you're okay, don't worry about the rest." Mike just stood there expressionless.

Sandy pulled him off to the side and looked him straight in the eye. "Is there something else you want to tell me? I'm here for you."

Mike embraced her again and stroked the back of her head with his hand. "It's…it's…"

"Go ahead, just say it." Sandy urged.

"I… I…"

"Yeah… You what…?"

"I went through all that to see Nathan, like…

like I promised, and… forget it, I'm tired. We'll talk tomorrow."

Sandy shrugged. "That's fine, but if you don't talk to me you're not doing yourself any good. It's better to let it out."

"I just want to go home now and sleep."

It was past one in the morning and Mike drove Sandy and his sister home and then returned to his apartment. He was exhausted. He undressed in the bathroom and took a warm shower. The water beating down was starting to diminish his tension but it wasn't enough to cool the circuitry in his stormy and tenacious imagination. That crazy man with the knife in the mouth still haunted him. The image flashed repeatedly behind his closed eyes with vivid detail.

He now regretted not telling the cops about it. The description of the van, the gas station, the man's features— all of it was freshly logged in his memory then and he had failed to do the right thing, like he always did. Sandy would be the deciding factor. He wouldn't gamble with her life. No way. If that maniac found out and came after her, then what? He had to put lock and key on the broken shackles of his racing mind. He needed to get some rest and put all decisions away until morning and then brainstorm a strategy.

Mike wrapped a robe around him and walked to the bed and sat down. Despite the fatigue draining the life out of him it was a chore just to lie down and close his eyes, let his thoughts drift away into a peaceful place. He sat staring at the walls around him, hoping that some clear and explicit resolution would write itself along the white sheetrock panels. He looked up at the ceiling and frowned. There wasn't a solution there either, just a fan with four blades that could serve a valuable purpose here and now; if he hung himself from them it would permanently erase the whole situation.

His thoughts descended from a dark and haunting diversion and landed on the phone sitting on the night stand in front of him. Each button represented a reason to him; a reason to dial the police and tell all he knew. It was the right thing to do, the next step in the process; so they can track the son of a bitch before he skips town and adds to the body count. He'll grab Sandy and escape another brush with danger.

He picked up the phone and held it to his ear. The dial tone hummed back at him. He reached out with his index finger and pressed 9. His face glistened with sweat and he wiped it away with the towel around his neck. When he swallowed it felt like a dry ball of sandpaper slid down his throat. He pushed 1. His index finger hovered, shook over the numbers. He thought of Sandy again—imagined that man's thick fingers wrapped around her neck, choking and squeezing the life out of her, her bones crumbling, and, as she died, her eyes rolling back in her skull. A vision of that razor sharp dagger shoved down her throat, or even his, offered the most horrid picture his mind ever scrawled. The series of revolting images kept shuffling and reshuffling and they would never depart unless he told his story to those who could apprehend the bastard now and lock him away.

He pushed 1.

It rang. The line picked up.

"Hello, 911, what is your emergency?"

The tears poured down his reddened face as he gathered breath to speak. "So sorry, I just woke from a bad dream and... and was shaken up, I... I apologize."

"Are you sure you're okay, sir?" the operator asked, unconvinced. "Calling 911 is serious business. Do you understand that?"

"Y... Yes, Ma'am. Goodbye."

After they hung up Mike wiped the tears from his face and went to the closet for his pajamas. He opened the door and grabbed a set from the shelf and walked to the bathroom to hang his robe. He put the terrycloth robe in place on the hook and a cool breeze grazed his left side. Mike turned and stiffened.   A plastic bag was sitting on top of the toilet underneath the window. Blood was seeping through the clear bag and dripping down the toiled bowl on the outside porcelain. He lumbered toward the bag and the curtain was lifted by the fierce outside wind. A track of blood ran from the bag, across the tiles, up the wall, and over the sill to the outside. He grasped the bag in his hands and began to unwrap it. His head was kinked away as he watched from the corner of the left eye. His hands shook feverishly. His head twitched while torrents of terror flowed through his body. The rain filtered in through the screen and peppered the tile floor. Mike stood barefoot with one foot on white tile and the other on a slick of cold blood. He came to the end of the bag and there was a *thud* as the contents dropped to the floor. His jaw gaped and his eyes opened into deep, hollow chasms. On the floor sat Officer Montoya's head with a piece of paper sticking out of the mouth. Mike reached down and pulled the paper out.

It was the *IOU* he had filled in. His hands trembled and his body started to tremor as the anxiety and uncertainty swam in his veins like poison. The paper slid from his grip. The IOU landed face down and there was something written on the backside. Mike collapsed to his knees and read the words in front of him in bold, black ink. A greasy thumb print underlined the letters. "Careful."

No One Survives the Holidays

planned a trip to Denver for Thanksgiving. The previous two years I missed out on our annual family gathering. Studying had taken over my life as I powered through Med School exams. Next stop was real-life cadavers and I hoped I could deal. "That's the true test," Professor Mcbain told me last semester. I made a promise to my mother to visit that year. No more excuses. It was always classes, friends, or my part-time job at the hospital that interfered with my family commitments. It was the time of year when students were in demand and, interestingly enough, when they were starving for cash. I sat in my dorm room with an open book in front of me. A pair of plane tickets was pinned under a mug full of pens and one of the Paper Mates was wedged behind my ear. My mother was stressed out and shouting into the phone.

"They don't quit, Becky! Uncle Jack has to take his pills at *just the right time* or he gets ornery. Aunt Dorothy's back is always out of whack. She's always in pain and complaining. Cousin Mike bitches that your father and I never visit him. Debbie whines that the turkey's dry and she's *never* pleased with dessert. She's a real ingrate! Then, after all of that hard work in the kitchen, they sleep on the couch until the next course. I'm so sick of it; so tired of putting on a show!"

Her voice was raspier than I remembered. Perhaps her love affair with cigarettes had flourished like my addiction to round-the-clock cappuccino binges.

I endured as much of her tirade as I could handle. "Why bother then, Ma, if—?"

She cut me off in mid-question.

"It's a tradition god damn it!" she cried out, he voice dark with anger.

I took a deep breath and exhaled while highlighting a few parts in my medical journal. "Look, I have to go, see you tomorrow."

The flight was grueling. We battled turbulence and I made frequent trips to the ladies room. Flying alone made matters worse. The guy next to me wouldn't shut up. My stomach was in knots from him going on and on about his computer job. I vomited a handful of times at my seat and filled three of those shallow barf bags. The plane was at full capacity. It was impossible not to feel constricted by the artificial air and the claustrophobic seating arrangements. The smell of sweat oozing from Mr. Talkative was enough to bring up the peanuts for a second taste.

The stewardess approached me and offered assistance. She had a spring in her step. She was a pretty brunette with all of about thirty years showing in her complexion. Her skin was without a blemish and she spoke with a voice smooth as silk.

"Anything you need, you poor thing?"

I pulled my head up from the barf bag and managed a half-hearted smile. "No, I'm fine, a little nauseous." The flight attendant put on a caring face for me. "I'm sorry, doll, we'll be landing soon."

I tossed an aspirin down the gullet and chased it with my ginger ale. "I know, it's just nerves," I added while discreetly pointing at the fat man next to me.

The stewardess chuckled.

I was about to take a sip of my soda when suddenly the plane dropped for the umpteenth time. "I hate flying and this plane is doing gymnastics," I told the attendant. "Plus, my Turkey Day is doomed. I'm visiting my relatives in Denver and my mother's already off her rocker."

The perky stewardess laughed harder as she refilled my drink. "Say no more, sweetie, I'm no stranger to that one."

The snack I'd eaten earlier worked its way up

my throat. I made a mad dash to the bathroom and plunged my head into the bowl. My voice echoed inside the tin toilet. "Please let me get through this flight…I promise, I'll put on a happy face, I swear. I'll let that guy talk my ear off all day."

I repeated those words over and over in my mind after losing my lunch twice more in the bouncing ladies room. I wanted to get off the damn plane. The pilot's deep voice spilled out over the intercom:

"We are making our final approach into Denver and should arrive within the next thirty minutes. The weather in the State Capital is thirty-five degrees with a crisp wind out of the North at twenty miles an hour."

I returned to the seat, wiped my forehead with

a wet napkin, and buckled up for the landing. Once the plane landed I called my mother and informed her that I had rented a car and was on my way. We discussed the brutal flight and how I needed a nap before company arrived.

"No problem, love, the bed will be ready for you," she told me.

I entered the house and saw my mother for the first time in years. The brown hair that draped over her shoulders was tangled with streaks of gray. Most of the excess weight she carried at the time of my last visit seemed to have melted away from her pack-a-day habit. She greeted me at the door with a big hug and a kiss while appearing uncharacteristically calm.

"This is a welcomed metamorphosis compared

to yesterday, Mom, and a good start to the holidays." As we broke our embrace I was still taking in the change.

"You're a whole new person, glad to see you so mellow." She looked at me with a twinkle in her eyes and beamed. "I've learned to let go. Your father taught me how to lighten up. That's why he's such a good business man. He never cracks under pressure."

I heard a *slam* and my dad approached from the basement door. He ran over and gave me a warm greeting. He hadn't changed much except for his waist. Last time I saw him he spent weekends on the golf course with the boys. He became acquainted with Jack Daniels according to my mother and his belly easily covered his belt buckle. We spent fifteen minutes or so catching up and discussing the rollercoaster in the sky that I flew in on. I finally settled in for a nap. I tossed and turned for awhile struggling to doze off. Being back in my old room again took some getting used to. It was just as I left it with only one small change: photos and graphs of the human anatomy had taken the place of some old family portraits. I found it refreshing that my parents took interest in my work.

I was a little overtired. Following a half hour of tossing and turning, I fell asleep. As I drifted off I still felt the after-affects, like I was trapped in that plane reliving the jarring experience. At least my stomach was slowly unraveling some of the knots.

Hours later a bad dream had troubled my sleep. I dreamt I was tumbling down a long, dark tunnel toward an inferno, and a voice was whispering in my ear telling me "It's just the beginning." The words repeated, again…and again. Beads of sweat dripped from my forehead and I saw a collage of disturbing images sweeping in and out of my sight. I saw my mother and father arguing about something and her screaming, "If you don't like it, LEAVE!" I saw my father storming out of the house in a rage and then my body became jittery. I felt my heart leap like a spring-board in my chest and in the midst of it all, I lurched forward in bed. My mouth stretched open to scream, a surge of breath got stuck inside my quivering lips, I was drooling and saliva was streaming down my chin in frothy strands. I started to dry heave and then I snapped out of it. When I came to I sucked in a few deep breaths to control myself. I glanced at the clock on the nightstand…7:00 P.M. It was a frightening dream and I felt relieved to be pulled out of that dark, terrifying place.

Why didn't Mom wake me for dinner? Oh my— I had been out cold almost three hours.

I flung the blankets aside and stood up. I was too embarrassed to go downstairs and engage with company before a warm shower and a change of clothes. My back-pack was on the couch in the living room and I had to get to it. I walked in a daze to the upstairs railing and listened for voices. It was quiet; I could hear my own heartbeat. My parents must have been in the back den setting up for company. I decided they must be going for a late start this year and it'll give me a chance to prepare myself. I went downstairs and grabbed my bag.

Suddenly, I heard something in the basement. A hair raising *POP* startled me. It was unusually loud, like the sound of an exploding balloon. Crackling from my parents' wood-burning stove, I thought. I darted to the cellar door and descended the steps to investigate the noise. When I reached the basement floor I smelled something awful. The stench turned my stomach. I covered my nose and mouth with my *Patriot Hills Medical* shirt. I walked carefully to the back of the dark basement and my face grazed a chain dangling from the ceiling. It frightened me. My instincts kicked in and I swung at the cord. The downward force snapped it. The room flooded with light. My eyes witnessed a reality that was beyond comprehension— a blood-bath. My relatives were butchered and piled up in front of the wood-burning stove. All of them mutilated, layers of skin peeled away. Next to the bodies was the electric carving saw and spare blades. All three of them coated with fresh bloodstains. Their flesh was pried open and the insides were gutted.

"Soon they will be kindling for the fire," Mom's voice declared from behind me at the crest of the stairs.

I didn't want to believe what I was seeing. Aunt Dorothy's spinal cord was exposed and severed in three places. The bottle containing Uncle Jack's pills was stuffed into his mouth and Cousin Mike was buried underneath him with a paper crumpled in his mouth.

Clump...Clump...Clump. Mom came down the

rickety stairs wearing rubber boots and gloves.

"Now all of us can enjoy a stress-free holiday," she announced in a soothing timbre.

"I thought the directions to Cousin Mike's house, stuffed into his mouth, added a nice touch, don't you?"

I shuddered and shook my head in disbelief. I didn't know what to say, how to react? This kind of carnage I had yet to discover in medical school and I wasn't sure anymore if I could handle it. She placed her arm around my neck and guided me toward the stairs that ascended to the kitchen. I was too shocked to scream. My body went into lockdown. I was numb. I clung to her on the way up the creaky, wooden steps. My body was trembling, and my skin felt cold under my shaking hands that grazed my skin. My legs wobbled. I was dangerously close to fainting.

"C'mon, my baby, let me fix you a plate with all the trimmings."

Then she looked into my face, her eyebrows raised; a smile form ear to ear was accented with pearly white teeth despite her years of chain smoking. She embodied that cheerful disposition; the same one she displayed earlier today when I arrived.

"Let's go eat before Debbie gets here and spoils everything. And by the way, Christmas is right around the corner. Promise you'll pay us a visit."

Skinned Alive

Veronica stood in front of the mirror admiring her beautiful reflection. She possessed the rarest of traits, the kind only seen in the magazines similar to those spread out on her mattress. *Cosmopolitan, Star, Fashion World*, there were at least five different periodicals overlapping one another on the silk sheets, each of them overflowing with fashion secrets, makeup advice, and pages full of products from *Maybelline to Victoria's Secret,* all promising to enhance today's woman. She ran her hand through her long black hair that was painted with highlights of brown frosting. Her lips were full and red. She puckered and added layer upon layer, dabbing off the excess with a pastel colored kleenex. Veronica didn't need to apply eye shadow or mascara. With her immaculately manicured hands she smoothed out the imperfections on her skirt by riding her delicate hands along her hips and sliding them down a set of thighs devoid of even a blemish. A confident smile gleamed from ear to ear. Her eyes traveled— and admired— every bodily feature from her silky-smooth hair down to her costly pedicure.

When she opened the closet door her fingers massaged her temples to ward off the stress of complementing her beauty with "shoes to die for." That phrase was a staple of the Veronica persona. Five minutes passed. Her hands remained in place rubbing out the pressure of such a monumental decision in a woman's life. After careful consideration she opted for a pair of open-toed suede pumps from Bloomingdales and slid her feet into them. Then a spin to the right— and one to the left— assured her they were the correct choice.

Veronica ran to the girl's room for one last primping before going into public. On her way to the bathroom she flipped on the television and the set erupted with a report from the news channel. A newscaster shouted from the set. "Ladies and gentleman, the horror lingers! There are five confirmed to have been exposed to the outbreak and four more are reported in critical condition, but doctors say they *will* survive!"

She ignored the newscast while admiring herself in the bathroom mirror, giving her lips one last pucker before the road. The ample overhead light highlighted her perfect features—she was glowing inside. She emerged from the ladies room, grabbed her purse, and carefully inspected the contents. Mirror—check, lipstick—check, mascara—check, eye shadow—check, remedy for a pantyhose run—check.

In the background the reporter droned on about a girl burned in a near fatal car accident: she had lived through the trauma but would be permanently scarred for life. They wanted to interview the semi-conscious young woman but communicating amidst the tubes in every bodily crevice was impossible. Veronica strutted to her apartment door with her fingers raised to her mouth, blow drying her nails.

Once her foot touched 27th Street she turned it on. She *knew* she was irresistible. She worked the street as men bobbed and weaved to attain a better vantage point at Veronica Myles. Her allure was instant, her spell captivating. Men leered. She was the bait, and testosterone-driven males were hungry sharks feeding like they'd never eaten. None of them had a chance at procuring a *roll in the hay* and she crafted her game like a veteran player. She floated down 27th ready to flag a taxi to a meeting with an executive named Christopher T. Rawlings, a real financial powerhouse with a high patience threshold. She was late for a meeting last week with him, but he never made an issue of it.

"Life's too short," he always said.

It was amazing to watch the cabs compete for her. On a good day a cabbie would waive the fee or cut the rate in half to earn a scrap of her affections. A black and yellow pulled to the curb to pick her up. For no apparent reason she looked down the street, 3rd Avenue, and spotted a digital billboard scrolling propaganda about a new line of perfume that guaranteed, *Men won't know what hit them!* Veronica's priorities suddenly changed and she waved off the cab. "Rawlings won't mind," she told herself while making a beeline for *Lori Anne's Perfumery.*

"Where ya goin there, sweetheart?" the cab driver yelled with a delicious smile.

Veronica did not respond.

Third Avenue was a hub of activity. Breakfast carts were selling coffee and bagels, the smell wafting down the street, enticing the hungry pedestrians who waited in lines ten deep. Buses and taxis were staggered along the curb. Passers-by ignored the traffic signs and crossed the street to get food. A half block of traffic was attempting to pull down 3rd but was blocked by the herds of scrambling people.

Veronica slithered through the unruly crowd, found the front door to the perfumery and entered.

"It's about time." she groaned, wiping a trail of sweat from under her eye and flattening a wrinkle on her rising tight skirt. She scanned the interior of the store. Big screen T.V.'s were hanging from each wall, airing music videos and the sound pulsated throughout the place. Shelves at least six rows high were stocked with perfumes and lotions and snaked along the walls from one corner to the next. The walls were painted a soft yellow with pink and white dazzles of color adding an enticing feminine touch. At one of the display racks she spotted an attractive couple huddled together. The lady sprayed herself with a sample bottle of *Lust* and the man drew closer to savor the aroma. His eyes rolled back in approval and the couple shared a smile. Veronica envied their closeness, their compatibility, the need they expressed for each other with simple inaudible body language.

Veronica strolled up to the counter, and as she approached, a young clerk of about twenty- five greeted her. The sales associate exuded an innocence; it may have been her horn-rimmed glasses that magnified her eyes to the size of golf balls, or her frizzy hair which was tied back and devoid of style; a ring hung from her left nostril.

"Can I help you?" the clerk asked.

Veronica's smile broadened, displaying straight- white pearls of health. She pointed at the back rack where the couple sampled the perfume.

"Your *biggest* bottle of that, please."

"My pleasure," the assistant chimed as she bounced to the rear of the store.

Veronica stood bewildered that the girl had disappeared to the back when there were plenty of bottles out front. She slid over a few feet but a stand full of lipsticks impeded her. There were more colors than any woman could use in a lifetime, too much to choose from, so she decided on a handful of six for the road. The smiling cashier returned with a box in her hand and placed it gingerly on the counter.

"Anything else?"

"Yes…these too…that'll be all."

Veronica squinted, her eyes quizzical. "What is so special about this bottle?"

The cashier looked puzzled. "I'm sorry. I don't understand?"

"Well, you went to the back." She raised a hand over her shoulder toward the rack again. "There's plenty over there."

The cashier chuckled. "Miss, you asked for the biggest, right? They're kept in the stockroom."

Veronica was confused. "Oh. I could have sworn that... forget it."

As the lady handed Veronica her change and her receipt, she smiled deviously.

"One spray and you'll be fightin' 'em off, Miss!"

Veronica Myles arrived at the office. Before

she met up with Rawlings she dowsed herself with *Lust.* During the meeting it was as though he was at a loss for words; unable to concentrate. She had a power over him that she had felt with no man previously. The perfume overwhelmed him and the longer the session lasted the closer he moved near Veronica. The powerful fragrance she had misted on her skin just minutes ago cast a spell of sorts over him. She imagined what she would do with the rest of the bottle. It was still full. The trivial amount she used hadn't put a dent in her supply. The cashier wasn't kidding, she thought. I'm going to have to fight them off!

The stunning Ms. Myles used the alluring potion on at least ten more men, all with similar results. They were driven to her with an animal attraction. She was irresistible before, but now? She was unstoppable! This fed her ego further and that was the kind of endorsement she craved. That's exactly what those movie stars and models felt every day as their heads swelled from constant approval, and her mind bloated with the possibilities. She coated herself all day; the seductive odor drifted from her pores and cast its hypnotizing tonic freely. This was every woman's dream, and she was living it. She enjoyed watching men fall at her feet. Although she had never had problems attracting men before today, this discovery was too persuasive to turn away from.

Following a long day with her sidekick *Lust,* she walked wearily into her apartment to relax for the evening. Veronica Myles was exhausted. *Clop-Clop-Clop*, her high heels bounced from step to step as she ascended the staircase. She had never had so much fun. She enjoyed the rush she felt from the drooling men who fell under her charms. She knocked 'em dead all right!

Veronica began to wind down for the evening. She undressed and covered herself in a silk robe, then ran a hot bath. As the water swelled in the tub she sat on the rim sipping a glass of her favorite wine and reading the latest issue of *Celebrity Fashion Secrets*. A sucking sound oozed from the tub faucet. She shot her eyes in its direction. The water was flowing as it should, so she engrossed herself once again in the magazine.

Minutes later the tub filled. She reached to shut down the faucet when that sucking sound came to life again. It was louder this time and the water surged violently, creating a mass of bubbles. A scratchy voice permeated the room, swirled in her ears incoherently. It was a slow, drawling voice like the sound of a warped record. Veronica dropped her glass and the tile pooled with red wine. A piece of broken glass cut the top of her foot. She winced in pain. The gash created a diversion from the voices and the crazy water for a few moments. She cleaned the cut with a wash cloth, wrapped it in gauze, and went to bed.

She wanted to sleep, tried to sleep, but spent an inordinate amount of time tossing, turning, and shifting for a good position. The experience in the bathroom was an incident she purged from her mind. Veronica glanced at the wine bottle on the coffee table and wondered how a couple of glasses could affect her that way. Clearly that was the first time she had heard strange noises or watched the water run amok all by itself.

Midnight. She was in a deep sleep, finally. The apartment was dark except for a kitchen stove light that emitted a passive glow across the room, lighting the way to the bathroom. Her breaths were soft and profound, her chest rising and falling in a peaceful rhythm. Something suddenly kicked in Veronica's stomach, like the sensation of a baby kicking in the mother's womb. It forced her eyes open, yanked her from a deep sleep, lurching again with a more powerful thrust. Veronica wiped her eyes and turned toward her dresser. The clock flashed 12:03 A.M. She felt something weird inside her. Her eyes darted down and she saw her belly rise.

An entity of some kind took over and latched

onto her wrists, pulling them with a violent outward motion. She fought, resisted with all the strength her body could generate. Veronica felt her control, her thoughts, the air in her lungs, slipping away in an instant. Dizziness spun her equilibrium aslant, as if the room was on its own spool, winding and teetering in every direction. Her wrists began to be twisted around the bedposts. She couldn't stop it. The bones popped one by one. The pain was unmerciful. Her long fingernails became embedded in the wood but she was still fighting against this unknown force, trying to break free of its stronghold. She inhaled as deeply as she could and with a fleeting burst of energy she played tug-of-war with her own body.

Seconds passed, then minutes, and she dislodged her fingers from the oak posts. During the separation she began to scream, cry, and gag from the torturous feeling. As the nails left her skin the blood from the torn flesh drizzled in thin rivers down her forearms. Her legs kicked and flailed as if she was smothered and losing air. Her arms and hands unwound from their contortion and Veronica jarred her body loose from the bed, eyeing an escape.

Each step she took was thwarted by a presence rebelling against her progress. Her legs and arms felt heavy. Her head was throbbing with a pressure beyond any headache. She lumbered toward the front door and reached for the phone on the counter.

A dial tone. That gave her a shred of hope, but she couldn't speak. Only hoarse, dry air came out of her mouth. When her fingers got near the buttons to dial, Veronica bellowed with anguish. It felt like a dagger was shoved into her cuticles. She dropped the phone and it crumbled to pieces. The entity forced her, dragged her to the bathroom once again. She made it to the medicine cabinet and peered at her horrid reflection. Veronica Myles was unrecognizable: arms and hands a bloody mess, face white as a ghost, hands broken and mangled. She stood in the bathroom a beaten woman, sucked hollow of her life force and her will.

Suddenly, the bathroom door flew open and slammed three times in succession. She was hunched over in front of the sink. With a quivering hand she pulled the medicine cabinet door open. Veronica's eyes locked on the top shelf full of prescription medication, the bottom covered with blood-stained razor blades. The signs were all too familiar. The demon was drawing her in again. Her tattered fingers reached for a razor and then…

The entity thrust her across the room; airborne, she landed in the tub. The shooting pain was unbearable, but the demon wouldn't relent. It wanted her to suffer and fear, suffer and fear. That voice returned again, whirring in her ears. The demonic voice demanded, "I WON'T LET YOU DIE! YOU MUST FEEL IT! LIVE IT!"

Veronica could not respond: her eyes were partly closed, her skin cold and prickly. She felt her whole body going numb, but not quite yet. There was more to overcome and the demon ratcheted up its unwavering power. More pain delegated itself to her neck, then her chest, and the back. The agonizing sensation found residence in lesions all over her body. She felt a stabbing widespread under her skin. Her scalp started to split into sections as if sliced open with a surgeon's razor sharp scalpel. Then a fleshy tentacle of some kind tore its way to the surface, revealing a nail, then the formation of a grotesque hand. More of the gooey tentacles spawned all over her shapely figure from head to toe. When these talons punctured the skin they began to pry the flesh apart in all directions. Her skin became pliable like melting wax. Now her body was infested with talons doing the job of knives, carving, stripping away her outer shell to breed new life, to take over what lurked underneath her once eye-pleasing exterior.

12:30 A.M. Veronica Myles was splayed in the tub, shrouded in her old flesh and her skeleton covered in a mass of sludge. What used to be her face was now engulfed in slime. Any facial features were now obscured behind the marsh. Suddenly, an oval cluster of the gelatin mass gave way to expose an opening eye, revealing a bright white retina. The sucking sound flared up and the tub filled again. As the water level rose, Veronica's blood streaked the water in red streams. Once the tub began to overflow, the surge of bubbles resurfaced, stronger this time. The faucet dial came to life, turning, and the shower sprayed down upon her helpless body. The chunky remnants washed away and gradually a new form spawned.

The form was that of another woman, a unique woman with a haunting appearance. It was the face that distinguished it from others. The eyes were misshapen. The skin underneath drooped down to show the blood-engorged skin and veins. The mouth was malformed, the lips no longer intact and the teeth now a dark brown and cumbersome for the small opening. The ears had tufts of hair growing from the canal. The facial tissue was pock-marked with pale, green pimples. No medical genius could repair the metamorphosis.

Veronica miraculously came to and both eyes opened to a new world, one she had yet to confront. She awoke as if from a living hell and assumed she had dozed off in the tub. All the pain had gone away and she wanted nothing more than to push that nightmare aside. She looked down and the water was a sanctuary of soap and bubbles. She rose from the tub and dried herself off with a towel from the nearby rack. She pulled back her hair and tied it into a bun, then walked up to the foggy mirror. Veronica ran her tongue around in her dry mouth. Her palate felt different, but she didn't know why. She squinted with confusion and swiped away a swath of fog from the mirror. She wasn't prepared for what greeted her in the glass. Veronica screamed, surveying her hideous features in frightful disbelief. Tears sprayed from her eyes, she dry heaved, then bent over and fainted.

When she regained consciousness her body was sprawled on the bed again. Each wrist was tied to a bedpost with nylon rope and her legs were bound in the same fashion at the bottom of the bed. A mirror was hung on the ceiling and it offered her a gnarly view of the new Veronica Myles; the one she would live with from now on. Her stomach roiled with grotesqueness so she turned away and wept even harder. From the other room she heard a noise, like someone was sharpening a knife, *Zing-Zing-Zing*. The unsettling sound crept into the bedroom where she was held hostage without an escape. The filing ceased. She heard footsteps coming towards her. The sound of high-heeled shoes, *Clop-Clop-Clop* on the tile floor, and then quieter on the living room carpet. The overhead lamps fired to life and cast a sparse glow over her bed. A woman approached her with a long shaving razor clenched tightly in her fist, the shiny blade gleaming in the pale light. The woman was wearing Veronica's clothes and a strong scent of perfume drifted over to her. The woman looked familiar. It was the eyes that she recognized.

But who was…?

The reality slammed her in the face.

It was the cashier from the perfumery. Her appearance was dramatically altered. In fact, the longer Veronica stared at her, the clearer she understood the story her eyes were telling her. The girl was almost a dead-ringer for her. She had somehow stolen her features and Veronica was left with the total deformity of her face. The cashier knelt down along the bed, smiled at her.

"You think my work is easy? I'm far from done. I have just begun. Soon all of those like you will incur my wrath and—"

Veronica trembled. "Wh… wh… why?"

The cashier's voice fired back with hostility. "Spare me the plea, you superficial bitch! You're all the same, it's always about YOU! Well, not any more!"

Veronica's dilated pupils rolled in circles. Her rash of pimples pulsated freely.

The cashier spoke calmly. "As soon as my secret perfume poisons the rest that I have so cleverly selected, I will take over the world with someone you know quite well.

Does the name Rawlings ring a bell? He financed my entire experiment and you were the tenth victim in my game. You fell under my spell quicker than the others. This will bring me victory and it's that kind of result that Rawlings is awaiting to launch this little project of mine?

You were number ten in a row and that fulfills my obligation to him. He requested live specimens.

Now, I realize just how powerful witchcraft is and my spells are forever stronger. I watched and orchestrated your every move during the last twenty four hours and found new ways to channel my spirit, or should I say, funnel my devilish desires into your home, and you. The stage is set, my little Ronnie... unless you die."

Veronica was frozen. She couldn't speak, the words stuck to the lining of her throat.

"If you die, you don't live with what I've left for you, and that, my friend, voids my contract with your Rawlings friend, and puts an end to my game, but it was *exhilarating* to manipulate you. You can't imagine the rush unless you're actually the one in the driver's seat."

She placed the long sharp razor in Veronica's

hand and got in her face, an inch from touching her. "Hmmm...tough choice. I'll look you in this eye... both of them are truly repulsive. I'm so proud of my work! So, tell me, Ronnie... I like calling you that. Anyway, the choice is yours. Can you live like I've left you, or do you want to end your existence for the better of your species?"

The cashier patted Veronica on the chest. "I'll let you think about that one. Call me when you're ready."

The cashier strolled out of the room, into the kitchen, and waited. She started to laugh and then covered her mouth with her hands. Minutes passed and the cashier heard Veronica gasping for air.

She ran into the room. Veronica was lying on

the bed with the razor jutting out from her neck. A

puddle of perfume expanded on the floor.

"What a shame," she said.

Beyond the Dark Glass

A picturesque elevation called Barracuda Mountain soars into the clouds of the western most part of Pennsylvania. The steep rocky peaks are eye-candy for tens of thousands of tourists and locals. A variety of winding streams have cut and carved their way naturally, eroding a multitude of drainage channels into Pocono Lake. The mountain, however, is not for the weak. Whether visitors hike to the pinnacle or bike up the rough terrain, they must be ready for an outdoor enthusiasts challenge. Every once in a while the mountain range waves a red flag or two. At the bottom, before the ascent, there is an imposing sign attached to wooden posts. Written in red painted letters on a sheet of plywood it clearly states:

All Who Journey On Do So At Their Own Risk.

Most daredevils think twice before they continue. A few have been known to backpedal after reading the warning. A number of trails are labeled. A scattered few bike paths wind along deep drops and others are a safer bet snaking the robust greenery of the ground level. No onsite medical facilities exist. The nearest hospital is ten miles from the lowest point of Barracuda. All visitors must bring food and beverage with them. Concessions stands are nowhere to be found. To a handful the benefits are plentiful.

That's what Amanda felt for many years: the need to conquer something new; to satisfy a craving for danger in some form; to live on the edge. She had plans to visit the adventurers' paradise one day but she had been wrapped up in other affairs with little time for indulgence. The magazine she read on Barracuda stated that nature lovers enjoy the peak on the far- east side. Climbers that have stood at the precipice enjoyed the beauty of the sun setting or the illusion of the moon's closeness at night. They felt as though they could reach up and pull the glowing star right out of the sky with their bare hands— it just seemed that close. The bold light it shined produced dark shadows that flirted with the prickly mountain side. The article juiced Amanda up and brought back glimmers from the past, especially of being a teenager, the time when she discovered what it was she cherished so much; true life bonds that would last forever.

Amanda and Julie's friendship dated back to sophomore year in high school when they realized the undeniable chemistry they shared. After a while it was as though they finished each others sentences, their thoughts. Often that's exactly what Amanda had done. Julie found her friend's talent oddly amusing. She remembered one particular day vividly, during the time when she had a major crush on Steven Barker from math class. She watched and waited for the perfect opportunity to ask him out, or to coerce him into making the move. He didn't take the bait so she spoke to Amanda about it in the hallway after class.

"I need to ask you something, *Amanda Panda.* What should I—?"

Before she could fire off the rest, Amanda did it for her. "What should you do about Steven Barker? Go after him before someone else does, silly."

Julie really admired her friend's guts, and

hoped one day she would have that much nerve. They had spent a lot of time attached at the hip: riding bikes, shopping, gossiping about boys—the usual teen stuff, and they mixed in fun excursions from time to time. When most of the class was frolicking at parties, they were off in their own little world. Amanda was courageous and Julie always followed suit, went along for the ride. After graduation the duo occasionally chatted on the phone. They saw each other when their schedules could accommodate. Julie moved up west near the Poconos and Amanda resided in the southern tip of New Jersey. They maintained apartments and had busy careers.

Time flew by. The years washed away and dried up into a new decade. Julie met Mark, a savvy business man who traveled around the world as an entertainment manager. He was always in and out of town but they made it work. Amanda, on the other hand, remained single. She dated a few times but her tom-boy looks and briskness had never won her points with the high school boys, and now it was still slim pickings. She brainwashed herself to believe: *five foot two, meaty, muscular shape and a butch haircut isn't going to win her any hotties.* Amanda enjoyed her life nonetheless, working as a freelance sports writer for a local magazine kept her plate full.

A scorching summer day was on tap, the heat sizzling for almost six o'clock in the morning, the sun hardly at full-strength. It had not climbed far above the horizon but was already burning through the clouds. Amanda's bedroom was all about athletics. The large dresser across from the bed was lined with trophies. An enormous silk flag of Lance Armstrong was pinned on the wall. In front of the window her bike was attached to a stand surrounded by tools. She was lying in bed without the covers on, sweaty-faced; with strands of hair matted to her scalp. The air conditioner hummed but the humidity seemed relentless. She tossed and turned, moaned repeatedly, couldn't get comfortable. Her eyes began to roll under her lids and she started to mumble through clenched lips. Amanda began kicking her legs like a swimmer struggling to the surface, her movements wild and uncoordinated. Her lips parted slightly and words became audible.

"No... No...Oh no..." Her voice trailed off.

The words seeped from her mouth in a deep groan. Her hands rose to her head, grabbing clumps of hair, wrenching her head back and forth. Suddenly, a frightening vision assaulted her dreams…

She is riding her bike through the forest, pedaling at full speed, her legs grinding hard. Her muscles and tendons are throbbing sharply as she maneuvers around rocks, crushing sticks along the way. The bike avoids numerous boulders. She jumps over fallen trees that impede her path. The muscles ache so bad, hurt so savagely she feels like they are burning to cinders. She races for her life as short, shallow breaths burn her lungs, pushing herself to the threshold of endurance.

Ahead she sees a highway; she digs down deep to summon strength she never knew she had, blazing onward. She's riding like the wind as branches and trailing vines scrape at her arms and tear holes in her flesh. All types of thorns are needling her and embedding deep in her skin. She looks back and sees it hot on her trail a short distance away, trailing like a floating ghost, chasing steadfastly. It is so close. She is fifteen feet from the blacktop, sensing escape, pedaling with all that's left in her storage chest of courage. The front tire finally crosses the wood's edge and hits paved road. She navigates over the crest of the paved hill. She breaks away from that horrific black thing. A glance back reveals it's out of sight. She slows down and allows the breeze to cool her skin, rolling downhill. She prepares to pedal up a steep hill fifty feet ahead. Out of the blue a truck flies by and crosses over into her lane and slams into her. She is thrown into the air, over the hood of the truck. The impact is loud, crunching, like a suicide victim jumping in front of a train. Amanda watches the world go white, spinning down a psychedelic tunnel where body and bike are fused together in a bloody mess.

The clock on the end table was glowing: 5:58 a.m. The phone rang and jolted Amanda from her bad dream. She sat up against the headboard and caught her breath. The phone rang again and again. She glared at it with weary eyes. Who the heck calls at this hour? she wondered. Reluctantly she answered it.

"Hello, who is this?" she asked, ticked off.

"…Manda, it's me, babe, your long lost pal, Julie!"

Amanda was not amused. "Are you aware of the time?"

"Of course, I am. It's time for you to get up.

Besides, I know you always rise early for your six o'clock workout. Am I wrong?"

Amanda brushed off her comments and looked down at the floor at her gear. Running sneakers, sweats, and a spandex shirt were at the ready by the bedroom door. She had always stacked her clothes there the night before she rode. Julie invited her to Barracuda Mountain for the following week. Meanwhile, Amanda tried to recover from the horrible dream. That was a first for her, waking up in a pool of sweat and out of breath. It was only a dream, she told herself. Julie was persistent, anxious to see her friend again. It took some convincing to persuade Amanda. She was worried about a deadline with the paper that she needed to meet. After all the years Julie was wise to her friend's excuses.

"If your work is that important, bring it with you. I'll give you some space. It'll be like old times."

Amanda sat on the edge of the bed and glanced at a picture hanging on the wall in front of her. It was a photo of them together sitting on their bikes eating an ice cream cone out in front of *Dairy Delight* on Windsor Avenue years ago. That was their favorite place to cure a sweet-tooth when they were kids. The owner snapped the shot. A smile spread on Amanda's face.

"All right, Jules, I'm in."

Amanda arrived at Julie's on Monday afternoon. They settled in and relaxed, prepared to hit the trails on Barracuda the next day. Once the girls were together it was like old times and Julie was happy to see her friend going nuts on the mountain. They rode the trails, hiked through the gorgeous scenery, enjoyed barbecues and laughed about old times and growing up.

With so much ground to cover the week flew by and the girls had spent most of it touring the lower half of the range. They even explored some of the forbidden sections of the woods where strange items had turned up in the past. A woman last year had her bike tire popped rolling over some kind of animal vertebrae.

"It's been some week," remarked Julie, taking a mouthful of water, splashing some over her head and shoulders. "I didn't think I had it in me, definitely burnt off the Breyers from last night. Who'd have thought we'd polish off a half gallon?"

Amanda chuckled and then pointed uphill to another trail.

"Ready, Jules?"

Julie's jaw dropped. She wiped her brow with the left hand and raised the other in defense. "You must be kidding! I don't have it in me."

Amanda raised a brow at her. "You can do it. Just try."

Julie was hesitant, but lazily mounted the bike and pedaled awkwardly behind her friend. Today was the last day on the mountain for them. It had been a hot and wickedly humid week. Julie began feeling the aches and pains associated with the adventure. She wasn't as spry as Amanda, her drive had diminished. Since morning they had cycled from the base, gradually up the hills as far as their will would take them. They pushed and pushed, pedaled with vigor. Julie was riding along one of the trails, her tires crunching a patch of uneven terrain. It was a winding trail that hugged a forty-foot drop and at the bottom disappeared into a roaring rapid. Amanda was laboring at a higher elevation about a hundred feet away from her in a narrow path that was surrounded with trees. On the steep embankment to the left there were odd-shaped hairy roots jutting out from the crevices in the stone. Sections of the wall had spreading ivy flourishing, extending from a cluster of main branches that gave the drop a furry green shroud. The image was the money shot for the tourists.

Julie pedaled hard, exhausted. She tried to catch Amanda, who stormed ahead overzealously. Her vision became lazy, blurry, doubled; the sight of the trees and the lush landscape bobbing and overlapping. She reached for her water bottle. It was bone dry. Not so much as a drop to moisten her parched mouth. She was no longer sweating profusely. Her skin was tacky to touch, her body on the fringe of dehydration, in the throes of it, perhaps. A feeling of weightlessness forced her to stop pedaling and catch her breath. When her tired legs touched the ground the whole forest and the mountain range started to spin. She experienced a chilling sensation under the skin. The pulsating sun had drained the life out of her and she plummeted down the embankment.

She screamed loud, shrill. Her cries echoed amidst the hillside, filled the canyon. The bike tumbled wheel over wheel into the rushing river. It was hard for her to drown out the disconcerting thoughts in her mind. *Why did we climb so far up the hill where few wander? Why did I push myself so hard? Why did I pack so few supplies? Why me? What now? All I can do is wait and hope for help, clinging to the mountain like a spider.*

Amanda dumped her bike and scampered downhill, rushing to Julie's rescue. Her screams rose to a crescendo. She arrived at the jagged edge of the cliff and looked down. Julie was dangling halfway down the embankment, clutching desperately at the roots of a tree. Amanda sprung into action. She carefully crawled like a lizard as far as she could down the slope and spotted an old tree stump within range. It was all there was to use so she swung her legs over and wrapped her feet around the trunk. They locked hands. Julie was ridden with panic, her hands shook, her knuckles turned white from the constant pressure, the firm grip.

"Julie, I need you to calm down, okay?"

"But I'm—"

Amanda looked her in the eye. "I know you're scared. But just listen to me!"

With their hands entwined Amanda pulled with all her might. Julie clawed with her feet to gain traction, pushing upward toward flatland. Chunks and dust from loose rock broke off and showered down into the vast, hollow canyon. Amanda pulled harder, her breathing quickened. Julie grappled against the wall, climbing, propelling her body toward the top. She gained, inch by inch. Finally, Julie reached the stump and pulled herself to safety. Amanda collected herself and followed.

The two sat in the shade and took a deep breath.

"Damn, that was close, you could've been killed, Julie."

Amanda pulled her in close and hugged her. "I'll never leave your side again."

A cool breeze drifted in from the southeast part of the hill. Amanda handed Julie what remained of her water supply and her friend sipped it slow and easy. When they were able to move on Amanda rose and helped Julie to her feet. They called it a day and went back to Julie's place.

Her house was quiet and quaint. They sat at

the dining room table sharing a bottle of wine while Celine Dion's voice belted from the living room stereo. Containers of Chinese food were at the center of the table. Julie dropped her chopsticks into an empty box and pushed it away.

"I'm full."

Amanda continued nibbling on her vegetables. The open kitchen window permitted a cool, soothing breeze to float in, the curtains puffed into pillows. Julie leaned over and pulled an empty chair closer and picked up her purse, pulling out a pack of Marlboros.

"You smoke?" Amanda asked with a hint of condescension in her voice.

"Gimme a break, will ya. It's only been like a year, ya know. You have to try a little of everything sometimes, sample the menu."

Amanda smiled. Julie recognized those famous dimples right away. Celine Dion gave way to the rapid-fire angst- ridden melodies of Alanis Morrisette. "Love this one, totally cool album," Amanda interjected during *Jagged Little Pill*. Julie explained that WHKT in Philly is a killer station during the week, especially the weekend when they play a wide variety of rock-n-roll chicks. The conversation segued to old times. The girls piled back deep into the early years they remembered so fondly, rehashing some high school stories: weekends at the beach, crashing the football team's victory party and telling off the queen-bitch cheerleader, Dana Freedman. They shared a lot of life and after all that time apart they had never missed a beat. No matter how far apart they were the relationship they had withstood the miles between them. Julie dabbed out her cigarette in an ashtray and sat Indian style in the chair.

"So, how's your love life, Amanda?"

"You mean the lack thereof?" I didn't get what you have, Jules: the dark skin and the high cheek bones. I mean…I see where this is headed."

"Oh come on, stop it. I bet—"

She cut off Julie's lecture. "Actually, I get Keanu twice a week."

Julie furrowed a brow, puzzled but amused at the same time. Her hands rose and covered her mouth, her eyes widened with surprise.

"My romantic evenings, hmm, let's see. Friday and Saturday night consist of watching *Speed* on DVD. Then I take a cold shower."

Julie laughed off the comment. Amanda looked away forlornly. The guy-talk weighed heavily on Amanda, evident by the way her head drooped toward the floor. The room filled with an uncomfortable silence as the gals sat across from each other, each waiting for the other to speak. Julie reached across the table and tapped the surface softly with her hand. "Mr. Right is out there waiting ya know, Amanda. Any guy would be lucky to have you. When the moment hits, don't let it slip away, babe."

Amanda's sense of humor returned with a twinge of sarcasm.

"You're a sweetheart, Jules, thanks. I'll keep my eyes open. When the moment strikes, you'll be the first to know."

Julie rose from her chair and approached her friend with arms wide open. They embraced. "It's so good to see you again, *Amanda Panda*. And by the way, thanks for saving my sorry ass today."

"Wow, you haven't called me *Amanda Panda* since what, sophomore year? I love that name."

"I love you too, girl."

For five o'clock in the afternoon on a summer day the sky had threatened with gray clouds. A storm loomed large on the gloomy horizon. Julie watched her friend load a duffle bag into her trunk. She attached her mountain bike to the roof of the car, securing the locking mechanism. A quick stroll to the front and she tossed her purse on the passenger seat. Amanda peeked at the charcoal-gray sky and shook her head, uneasy. She realized it was only a matter of time until the sky opened up and dumped on her in her travels, but she had to go. Julie urged her to stay as long as she wanted. Amanda had an article to write so she was set on taking off. Two cups of espresso were swimming in her bloodstream, she was ready for the long haul. With all in check she headed down the driveway and made a left onto the main road. She beeped the horn and waved goodbye to her long time friend.

There was a place on the Jersey border called Cavanaugh's, an eatery and a bar, and a favorite among the locals. Long distance travelers couldn't resist stopping by for a good meal and a drink. The large barn-like building was set off the main highway and a sign towered over the pines before exit 61. Cavanaugh's was the last chance to eat for at least fifty miles. Rest stops and exits were scarce around that section of the interstate. The State Police hardly patrolled the area, only passed through once in a while to nose around.

The place was always hopping. The after work crowd had filtered in. Patrons sat around and watched the wall-mounted televisions that broadcast news and sporting events. A man sat on a stool at the bar wolfing down a few shots, his head resting in his palms, fingers massaging his temples, tiredly rolling his head in circles to loosen the kinks. Following the next shot his head dropped onto his folded arms resting on the bar. His eyes closed.

The man started to recall the tragedy that struck him only a week prior. The power of Jack Daniel's worked his mind, told him the gruesome details of a dark tale he wanted desperately to forget, pieces of a pure horror puzzle laced themselves together:

He had been driving down a deserted highway at night, his vehicle cruising along at fifty or so; he was in no rush that evening. Then he heard the rumble of motorcycles gaining ground behind him. He steered into the right lane allowing the bikers to pass. They stayed behind him, flicking their high beams and weaved in crazy patterns, toying with him. He was getting annoyed, patiently waiting for them to pass and be on their way. The lights on the hogs were blinding.

The bike gang sped up and stayed even with him. The gargling of the motorcycle engines was like thunder in the clear, once quiet night. Suddenly one of the bikers threw a lit cigarette that pelted his window, startling him, angering him. The clan raced ahead and cut in front of him, rode in tormenting circles, just feet from his grill. He ran out of patience. He put his hand out the window and flipped off the bikers, shouting at them, brimming over with anger. "Screw you, man!"

The pack tore up the road speeding from him as he tried to suppress his rage, but he couldn't.

"Yeah, that's right, drive away, jerk-offs!"

Their tail-lights faded away into the dark. A few minutes later he had to take a leak; between the liquor and the idiots on the road he was ready to burst. He pulled over to the shoulder of the road. He shut off the lights and found a tree to conceal himself. He stood behind the tree and enjoyed the feeling of emptying his bladder; his head tilted back, eyes closed. Strange the time that nature calls, he thought. He couldn't seem to get that piece of ass out of his mind, though, the one he boned hours ago, the hot waitress from Billy's place. She played hard to get but he weaseled a way in, he always pulled it off.

He heard a branch snap behind him. Brush rustled nearby.

Crunch...Crunch...Crunch.

He turned to the left as far as he could. Nothing. He turned to the right. Nothing. He couldn't stop the flow of urine, it kept on coming.

Clomp…Clomp…Clomp…Clomp.   A noise from behind him closed in. He tried to shake out the rest and get the hell back on the road. Something hooked a clump of his hair and tugged him backwards with whiplash-like force, the grip strong, powerful. He yelped in pain. He struggled to free himself but was overmatched.   A deep, gravelly voice spoke into his ear.

"Say it ta my face booy." The breath was foul, it made his stomach twist. The sickening stench was a mix of Slim Jims, cigarettes, and poor hygiene, perhaps. As he was dragged backward a stream of piss paraded down his leg, he was unable to pull up his pants, stymied each time he tried. The sweaty palm slid from his scalp and ripped a few hairs out with it, the hair tangled in the rings on the attacking hand. He

spun around and got a good look at the assailant, that biker nut from before. He thought fast and head-butted the fat man.

Crack. The biker's nose broke with the force of the blow. A cut opened on the nose and the biker fell to the ground, bellowing in pain.

The motorcycle maniac was pissed. "I'm gonna make you my bitch, booy, ya hear me?" He growled while a mist of spit flew from his mouth.

He heard a Click, then a Smack.

What the fuck was that? he wondered, frightened.

Something solid was pushed into his temple. A calm, female voice told him not to move. He knew it was a gun when he heard the barrel pin pulled back.

He pivoted slightly and saw a dykish chick holding a revolver. The fat man rose to his feet and unzipped his pants. The feeling of horror overwhelmed him. He had a gun to his head and feared what was in store for him. The nozzle of the gun was shoved, poked into his skin, again, again and again; a forth, fifth and sixth time. His head throbbed. He was weakened and alone. The raspy female voice commanded him. "Yer sorry ass is gonna give it to Edgar the way he likes it...in the ass."

Tears streamed down his face, he cried in silence. The ache inside him swelled and churned like a drill.

"Ya got till three to make up that mind a yers, or I'll do it for ya."

He trembled, felt his lungs losing air, total shock owning his every breath, every thought. The biker was bent over, ready and waiting for him to follow her instructions. If he didn't heed the warning he would feel a bullet spear a hole in his head.

"I'm not fuckin' around, just try me ya pretty boy piece of shit, clock's tickin'."

Her countdown began.

"One." His mouth swallowed a heavy flow of tears. Snot poured from his nose. He was drenched in his own sweat.

"Two." He held his left hand in the air, a plea for release. No chance. He felt the barrel jabbing into his bleeding temple, it twisted back and forth like she was screwing it into his head. What choice did he

have? Live? Die?

There was nobody around to save him. "Please, let me go!" he cried out, but his words only drifted away and meant nothing to the crazed bikers.

"Thr—"

The man's head snapped up from his folded arms on the bar.

"Wake up, McBride!" the bartender shouted while filling a drink at the tap.

"Oh, sorry, man; must have conked out for a minute of two. How about a shot of Tequila, I'll be good as new."

She hit the button on the CD player: 7:45 P.M.

Amanda had been on the road for hours. The high from the double-shot of caffeine earlier had diminished. She was exhausted, a little tense behind the wheel. Her eyelids were heavy. A few times her attention wavered and nearly got her in an accident. She had the music at number six on the dial, loud enough to keep her alert, she figured. It was dark and rain pounded the roof intensely, sounded like someone was drumming on it. The storm commenced about fifty miles back and had grown incrementally stronger, the winds hyper, difficult to drive in, blurring the road ahead of her.

She stopped the car on the side of the road, put on the hazards. The highway was practically dead, not much within eye range. She sat and imagined being home with a CD in the player, a hot cup of tea, and finishing her article that was due. Amanda spotted a faint light in the rain. She stared longer, sensed her luck was about to change. She peeled her foot from the accelerator and rolled along the shoulder to get a better view. She discovered an exit with fuel and food. At the bottom of the sign it read, *Last exit for the next fifty miles.*

Earlier her stomach had done its lion's share of growling. A hot meal and some coffee sounded like a good idea all of a sudden. She rode along and got off at the exit onto a quiet street. She stayed to the right and a white sign jumped out at her through the downpour.

Welcome to Cavanaugh's Restaurant and Pub. Underneath the welcome line, the phrase *Family Friendly* danced in a spectrum of color.

The lot was packed all the way around the eatery. A wooden fence encased the property and one long row of cedar trees caressed the fence-line on the opposite side. Amanda managed to steal a spot in the back next to a dumpster. She reached in the back seat and grabbed her trusty umbrella out from the door console. She walked briskly toward the main entrance and passed a herd of smokers lighting up outside.

Inside, the double doors sealed behind her. The establishment was pleasant, as she expected it to be. The left side was where the bar was situated. Old, rustic wooden tables were packed close together, filled with patrons. Straight ahead, dead center in fact, sat a long rectangular bar with the televisions hung from a wooden façade, outstretching the dangling glasses. How the hell can they hear the television over the loud conversations? she wondered.

A pretty, perky brunette strolled over to Amanda with her hair curled up in a bun and a navy blue shirt hanging over her low-rise black pants.

"How many do you have in your party, Miss?"

Amanda shot her a look. The hostess phrased her question with an inviting tone but it was the weird look that irked Amanda, the look of pity. She was probably thinking, *A woman...alone? Eating out on a Friday night?*

"Just one tonight, Miss," she replied and rolled her eyes.

The hostess guided her to a table and left her a menu to peruse. Amanda scanned the layout curiously. Over twenty antique-looking fans purred overhead, the wooden propellers spinning, softening the air. Rows of solid support beams crisscrossed in both directions, holding up the vaulted ceiling. On the far side of the place, catty-cornered, was an old phone booth.

The opposite side was home to a wide counter where the cash register sat. Shirts, hats, and sweatshirts embroidered with the restaurant's logo were stacked neatly on glass- enclosed shelves. Amanda wondered who would buy something like that, kidding herself that they probably sold a bundle to the people who drink all night and forget where they were the night before.

She pictured little kids tugging at their parents' shirt for the threads too. She nursed a hot cup of coffee and cleaned up the remains of her apple pie. She had the coffee mug clenched in her palm while looking around the place. A pair of plumbers was sitting at the bar with at least two empty drafts in front of them, a new one in their hands. Their white work shirts read *Marty's Plumbing.* She tried to guess which one was Marty, the one on the left with his crack showing and the crew cut, perhaps. Her eyes scrolled to the right a little farther and…

Wow! she thought.

She slowly lowered the cup of joe from her mouth onto the table. She was smitten. Her eyes engaged with a man that stood a mere twenty feet from her. The first thought that came to her mind was, *That is the sexiest man I have ever seen.* A rugged man, a shy, innocent face; smiling and staring at her. He was tall, dark and devastatingly handsome.

Her eyes darted away for a split second and she undressed him in her mind. A cool, tingly sensation fluttered in her pelvis. Was this the feeling that had eluded her all her life? Did she really possess the ability to attract a man like that? Out of the corner of her eye she saw him checking her out. She eyed him again as he sustained the same pose, then pointed at himself and mouthed, "You mean, me?"

He signaled the bartender and minutes later made his way over to her table holding two coffees. He placed one in front of her and the other in front of the empty chair. He extended his hand. "Name's, Wade, Wade McBride."

His smile was gentle, disarming. As she cradled his hand she enjoyed the thickness of it, the masculinity. He had the aura of a gentleman, clearly a man who had seen a lifetime of physical labor. This Wade must know how to treat a lady, she imagined. When her blushing subsided they spent time talking about everything from small town life to the nasty weather. They went through more coffee and dessert. The storm battered the rooftop, the sound of it drilling so hard and steady, relentless. She glanced over his shoulder and watched the streams cascade down the windows. There was no shortage of girls around the bar licking their chops at the sight of Wade McBride. Amanda noticed all of the admiring glances and ignored them as much as she could. She was flattered by his interest in her.

He finished the rest of his coffee and leaned back in his chair. "I'm going outside for a smoke, care to join me?" The one thing she hated— even though her friend smoked.

She remembered Julie's advice. *You have to give a little sometimes. Don't let it slip away when you find it.* Such powerful logic and reasoning.

"No thanks, Wade, but you go ahead."

"All right then, be right back."

From her seat Amanda saw a striking blonde, mid-thirties, sneering at her. Was the strange girl jealous of her, stunned at his selection of women? Amanda deflected with pride the sharp arrows of condescension the girl shot at her. She relished the moment, didn't want to let go of it. *Eat you heart out*, she thought.

When he returned from his smoke she realized it was late. They sat for a good chunk of the evening without a lull in the conversation. It was still raining, pouring. He placed his hands on hers. "Wanna split? Go to my place, maybe? At least it's quiet."

It came out of him nonchalantly. Boy is he smooth, she thought. When his hand touched her everything inside her became mealy. She felt her skin melt. Her cheeks blushed cherry-red. Her heart raced. Could she refuse him? She knew she had to get home but this was an unexpected and delightful detour. He inched closer and confirmed his intentions. "I live a few miles from here. We can have some tea and chill out."

Amanda sunk her hands discreetly into her purse. She had mace and a Swiss Army knife. If he tried anything stupid he'd lose his plumbing.

"Okay, Wade. But I'll follow you in my car."

He raised his right hand like he was being sworn in. "Whatever you want. It's your call."

Outside they stood underneath the overhang that ran along the front of the restaurant. It jutted out ten feet from the wooden walls and spaced strategically along the decking were old milk pails, various flower pots, and wind chimes hung from the rafters.   Wade and Amanda stood there for a few moments while he pointed out his truck. The rain angled in on them. They heard it knocking on the gutters above them. *Ping...Ping...Ping.*

"You see that baby over there? That's my pride and joy." She was impressed by his enormous truck. A large red four-wheeler elevated from the ground with a set of stainless-steel steps to climb; a real mammoth. A length of fog lights were attached atop the cab with a large spotlight in the center. They were about to run to their vehicles when a police car pulled into the lot. It cruised past the front and Wade threw his hand up to wave at the patrolman. The officer did not return the courtesy and Wade seemed taken aback. The policeman parked next to her car. Wade hustled to his truck and Amanda to her car. She grabbed a hand towel out of the glove compartment and wiped off her face and neck. The cop turned on his interior light and poked his head in her direction. She threw her purse on the passenger seat and looked up; saw the officer's plain-faced, emotionless stare. The rain dowsed his window. She saw the shoulder badge pushed up against the window, distorted. She drove forward where Wade waited for her. Amanda beeped her horn, signaling her arrival and they exited the parking lot.

They pulled up to his ranch, a spacious piece of property with a chain-link fence surrounding it. He parked in the driveway and Amanda parallel parked along the curb. They walked up several steps onto a porch. A rocking chair sat on the right side of the door with a set of fishing poles, a tackle box and a duffle bag against the wall. He unlocked the door and entered first, holding it open for her to come in. She was impressed by the layout; it had that country feel to it, warm and cozy.

"What can I get you, coffee or tea?" he asked politely.

"Tea would be fine," she answered as her eyes

roamed the interior.

Wade put the kettle on the stove and Amanda took a gander at the wall clock.

"Why don't you relax in the living room and I'll be right there."

She stood in the other room: a couch behind her, a television in front of her, a love seat to her right, set back, and an armoire filled with rifles in the corner. A large plaque hung above the mantle: *License to Carry Handgun.* When he walked into the room it all happened so fast. She simply gave in. Wade slid the purse from her shoulder and flung it onto the love seat. Amanda had hunger in her eyes and he sensed it. A small part of her wanted to stop him. After all, it was just some stranger from a bar and she had to get home.

There was an attraction and she knew she didn't want to fight it. But it was too late to back off as he kissed her neck and ran his lips up to meet hers. Her legs buckled, weakened. She tried to peel away his flannel shirt but he pushed her hand away and picked her up off her feet, carried her to a bedroom. She landed on a mattress and the lights went out. The storm, the darkness, the smell of him— it all seduced her and she surrendered to him. He removed her clothes one garment at a time until her bra remained. She could feel that he was still fully dressed. She honed in on the rain's drum roll on the roof, the ambiance. She tried to peel off more of his clothes but he took charge. They were in the blindness of passion. She wrapped her arms around him and clawed at his shirt almost tearing a hole in the fabric. She let go of her inhibitions and enjoyed his aggressiveness.

When they were done he slipped under the covers. She asked for the bathroom and he told her to follow the night light on the wall. "It'll be on the right." he explained.

Amanda sat on the toilet and her attention drifted around the room. The layout was typical, but not at all sloppy like most men's quarters, she thought. When she was through she cleaned up at the sink. On the right hand side there were storage shelves comprised of five different levels, all filled with a variety of toiletries. The top shelf stored towels, the second, soaps and shampoos, and it was the third that she found peculiar. At least five different medicine bottles struck her as odd, large ones with white labels.

From the bedroom Wade shouted, "Is everything all right in there?"

Amanda scrambled for a quick answer. "Y... Yes, be... be right there, Wade, just washing the makeup out of my eyes!"

Her head started to spin with a multitude of questions. What was in the bottles? Should she look? Is that the right thing to do considering she didn't really know this guy? She decided to play it cool and head back to the bedroom. She opened the door and walked down the hall. The light had been turned on. The storm weakened, she no longer heard it slamming the house. Amanda was eager to collect her clothes and be on her way. She was ten feet from the bed when their eyes met and suddenly an uneasy feeling washed over her. It was the look in Wade's eyes that alarmed her. They revealed no emotion; it was a complete and mysterious change from before. There was no sign of the man she had met just hours ago.

Wade yanked the blanket from his body and Amanda jumped back in horror. His lower body was infested with a rash, an oozing rash. The bubbly sores covered his genitals and spread up toward the waistline, invading the skin nearby. Some of the skin was peeling away and there were small sacks around his belly button. She flashed back to the living room; the way he forced away her advancing arm from removing his shirt and during sex how he kept his clothes on and shut the light off instantly. *Why did he do this to me? What provoked him?* How did she not feel the lumps inside of her? None of it mattered now, she was in deep shit and had to get the hell out of there, but she felt a new level of anger consuming her.

"You son of a bitch! How could you?" she yelled.

He was sprawled on the bed with a grin on his face. The gentleman she met had disappeared and a new demented Wade McBride had been spawned.

"You couldn't have known how it felt, you dumb bitch, what I had to do to survive, and all for what," he asked, pointing to his infection… "This?"

"What does that have to do with me, you evil asshole?"

He looked at her and hesitated, as if he was searching for an answer.

"Well, because you're her mirror image; and

the both of you look *butch* to me."

His explanation meant nothing to her. She felt the walls closing in on her fast. She wished she had a gun. She'd blow his damn head off right then and there. Amanda recalled the gun rack but knew if she made a break for it he'd be on her ass. She stood seething next to the bed, staring at his grotesque body. Her heart shuddered, her hands trembled feverishly. She hated him for being so manipulative and herself for being so gullible. The question repeated itself over and over again in her mind. *Why didn't I just go home?*

Whack. She lashed out, slapped him right in the face with all of her strength. She couldn't help herself, she felt so violated, stricken with who knows what life altering illness. Her hand struck his head and drove it hard into the headboard, leaving a red brand on his face. She broke the skin and blood dripped from his left nostril, his eyes filled with tears of rage. Hostility creased his face, his top lip quivered as beads of sweat formed on its ridge. He lurched forward. She ran around the bed to avoid his pursuit. She grabbed a picture frame from the dresser. He was closing in with his arms extended, to choke, to maim. She fired the frame at him and it struck his head, the glass shattered, some of it spraying him in the face. He teetered. Amanda was amazed at his resilience. He didn't fall. She ran straight for the door and he gimped after her with his hand to his bleeding face. She had no time to grab her clothes, she barely had time to think. He struggled to the front door and watched her speed off. He stood in the kitchen with blood drizzling down his face and saturating his shoulder. Amanda was off like a shot in the night. She followed the sign back to the highway and never looked back.

Meanwhile, Wade got dressed and hustled outside to the truck. At the bottom of the stairs he stopped in mid-stride and his eyes looked over his shoulder. A sadistic smile widened on his face and he walked back up to the porch and opened the duffle bag. He pulled out a machete from the bag and removed it from its sheath, gliding his finger along the edge, picturing the pain he planned to inflict on Amanda. The first incision would be his favorite: watching the blood seep from the wound and hearing her pain laden cries of agony.

She was driving madly and fought to keep the car under control. She sensed her danger was far from over. She tried to calm herself while many dangerous scenarios ran rampant in her mind. Will he find her? What pathogen is roaming in her body? She checked the rearview mirror just as head lights cracked the darkness in the distance.

A noise under her car, first a *pop*, followed by a louder sound, alarmed her. Then a cloud of smoke billowed over the hood, almost blinding her. Suddenly, she lost control of the car and careened off the highway. She collided with a tree and the screech of crushed metal bending and twisting created a cacophony in the night. The contact thrust her airborne and into the windshield, she fainted on impact. Beneath the car gasoline leaked from the punctured tank and crawled toward the front. Sparks flew from the dented hood. If their paths crossed body parts and steel would erupt like a volcano. The truck behind her stopped. One of her headlamps was smashed to pieces, malfunctioning. The other was cracked and its beam shined into the thick woods. A man approached the car and witnessed Amanda, vulnerable on the front seat and unconscious.

The driver's side door creaked open...

She gradually awoke and the first thing her eyes opened to was a faint light overhead. Her head was throbbing and the pain worsening, it blurred her vision. She looked down and saw a blanket cocooning her body. A voice spoke. The sound of static leached from the front seat.

Click. "Mackellan's to dispatch, you there?"

A short pause.

"This is dispatch, go ahead."

Click. "Got a girl with me, she was in a bad accident, takin' her to the hospital. (He coughed hoarsely). Better notify State Police, do you copy?"

Another short pause.

"We're on it, she got a name?"

Click. "Don't know, man, she's got no I.D, purse, nothing. I found her nude for Christ's sake."

Another short pause.

"Ten four."

Amanda was propped against the door of the king cab and through the crack of the seats she saw part of the driver. He had long hair in a pony tail and an overgrown goatee.

"Just relax, dear, getting you some help," the man said.

She scanned the cab to gain her bearings. The roar of his diesel engine vibrated the interior. On the floor behind the seat were ropes and chains with hooks fastened to them; mounted on the back sliding window were racks that held tire irons and pry bars. A pack of cigarettes sat in the center console. The glove compartment was open and she noticed a flashlight, papers, and an empty beer bottle inside. She studied his shirt, read the patch on his shoulder.

Mackellan's Contracting Inc.

24 Hour Service.

Suddenly a piercing light sliced through the darkness behind them. It was a ways back but closed in fast, now five hundred feet away. Amanda recalled the strip of lights at the top of Wade's cab. Dryness sealed her throat. Fear rendered her defenseless. She was not on the mountain where her expertise kept her sharp, instinctual. This was danger she never planned for. Her complexion was pale, withdrawn. The driver shut off the overhead light. That truck was gaining, it was on their tail. It was a hundred and fifty feet away, closer, a raised truck with gigantic tires, it towered over the road. She fought to catch her breath. She clamped her hands over her mouth.

"Take it easy, honey, we're almost there," the driver assured her.

Amanda savored the one shred of hope; maybe he wouldn't see her behind the dark glass, the tinted glass. The truck was twenty- five feet away and closing in. She remembered the lion like sound of Wade's engine and the nickel plated tool box that gleamed in the light of the cargo lamp above it. The truck was side by side with them. Her body shook. She was so frightened. She felt the urge to defecate on the seat. Amanda couldn't see the driver but the truck was an indelible memory. It could never be erased no matter how long she lived. The trucks were rolling side by side for almost a mile and the murmur of tires spinning thousands of revolutions and the diesel engines rumbling in unison was all she heard. His powerful spotlight up top searched for her, whirled in every direction, tracking her. Wade's ray of light passed over the tow truck, but he couldn't detect her. Wade sped up ahead a safe distance and Amanda felt new life running through her. Her strength began to flourish again as his tail lights floated farther away, becoming small evil eyes looking back at her.

Things took a strange turn. Wade's truck came to a screaming halt. Friction from the tires created a smoke screen that camouflaged the road ahead. The truck stood at a stand still for a few seconds. Their truck approached his when Wade made a turn and crossed over a grass divider and headed in the opposite direction. Amanda swallowed dry air. She was fortunate her driver never lost his composure. He saved her life. She tasted home on the tip of her tongue. Soon she would be enclosed by the four walls that warmed and protected her. But for now her eyelids were tired and heavy. She needed sleep. She leaned back and closed her eyes once more but for reasons she didn't understand her mind shifted to that dark place again...his living room. A scary image swirled in her head at blinding speed. What she saw was real, a trail back to her. Amanda saw her purse— her identification, license, her life's blood— still sitting on his love seat. He would soon return home and find it. When that happened he would be armed with all a maniac needed to track her, and finish what he started. What she wouldn't give to hear *Amanda Panda* right now and maybe climb Barracuda with Julie again, perhaps…smoke a cigarette.

Mind Plays Tricks?

My engine finally turned over that morning. Thick, stubborn ice overspread the windshield. The temperature was well below freezing and the frigid weather was forecast to stick around through the entire week. When I fired up the ignition the digital clock on the radio spat out 4:30. That's way too early in the morning to be out on any day, let alone during an arctic spell. That's how it felt to me. The chill followed me around everywhere like a ghost. The boss was on the warpath. We had finished installing a roof over a week ago at Bayview and some big office building in Cedar Falls. We left a few residual supplies and scraps up on top and the tenant wanted them off before sunrise so he could show a unit of office space to a prospective client. I couldn't believe they pulled me out of bed for that crap but my superior called me from his warm bed and told me to get it done.

Next to me on the passenger seat was a fax that listed the job details. I had to get to the roof of the building and lower the items with ropes and a pulley system like we normally do and be out of there by six. The boss failed to keep in mind that after a minute outside your extremities are screaming for mercy. The car slowly warmed up and melted away the thicket of ice shrouding the windshield. An angry wind swooped down and swirled around my car; my Plymouth swayed. That must have been the winter ghost warning me of what I'll encounter on that roof. As the streams of water melted away and spidered down the glass all I could think about was being in my bed with a warm blanket as my cloak and guardian. Ah! Warmth and relaxation. The heat was blowing strongly and my sinuses started to clear. The remnants of the flu still tormented me but I had to get to work.

The crew and I entered the office complex and sat in our vehicles contemplating the next move. Another wind squall whipped through the parking lot, its whistle loud and fierce. There was a long row of pine trees, at least fifteen, perched up on the hill across from us, their limbs bending from the wind's torque. The moon hovered in the sky full and bright. I slipped into a trance that transported me back to an early spring morning: I was in bed. It was early and I heard a noise outside. I went to check it out, otherwise I'd never sleep, probably just stare at the walls all night. I opened the front door and walked onto the stoop.

Nothing. I raised my head to the sky and there was that full moon, painting the sky in cheerful colors that meant a warm day was on the way. That morning I eagerly waited for sunrise, knowing it would burn off the morning clouds, knowing the rising sun would deliver a glistening sweat to my skin. When I returned to bed my wife nudged me, never opening her eyes. She mumbled. Her dry lips squirmed out of synch. "Are you hearing things again?" she asked.

The cold lashed out and stung my face, stealing me from the trance as I stood outside the car. I hated to imagine the mind-numbing temperature at the roof and how little the conditions would help me overcome the battle with the flu. We walked to the front entrance where a few streetlamps gave enough light to guide the way, but with each strong gust of wind their bulbs flickered, danced. I peeked into the gigantic office windows, observed the dim lighting. I informed the others that when I reach the roof they would assist from the ground. Tim, Chris and Evan nodded in agreement while they rubbed their hands together and pulled up their hoods.

When I first entered the structure it all seemed normal. The heat felt good warming my limbs. I noticed the first-floor layout had been entirely rearranged, completely different from my last visit. To the right used to be a reception desk, now it was a pile of sheetrock panels, twenty or so stacked high. The interior itself was under major construction. Holes spread about the far walls. Shards of glass were scattered on sections of the floor, surprising for a work area considering how dangerous broken glass is. A pair of work boots sat next to a sawhorse with a stained shirt draped atop. Who would leave their clothes behind? I wondered.

For the time being I avoided the distraction and searched for a staircase, even an elevator. I crept through the room and turned the corner, which brought me face to face... with a knife, the blade buried deep in the wall. The handle was thick; the few inches of exposed blade had sharp, grisly teeth running along the bottom.

From what I could ascertain the wall was newly assembled, taped and spackled. *Why on earth would someone...?* I moved on. From the looks of it the room and hallways were nothing but a jumble of dark paths silently begging to be discovered. I swept through the corridor and encountered an elevator. I pushed the button to call it. No response. That's strange. The two lights on the control panel were glowing green. That was the easiest way to the hatch but I looked for an alternate way up. The long hall surrounding me was lined with rooms on both sides. I wiggled the doorknobs as I passed each one. All of them were tightly sealed. In a few places, where the walls intersected with the ceiling, I saw that a family of spiders had been busy tunneling out a home, storing trespassers in the crevices, on the prowl for other insects that roamed behind the dark walls, the nooks and crannies.

A room was nestled at the end of the corridor, the door ajar. I moved forward and opened it slowly. The rusty hinge squeaked. I took a few steps. Standing before me was a huge cubicle divider about six feet high. A night light at floor level cast a subtle glow and threw a shadow on the torn carpet. I flicked the main switch to my right and from the florescent tubing above, the room filled with light, grungy and faint.

Curiosity beckoned me, drew me in. I circled the room, explored. Something on the back floor needled my spine. Goosebumps broke out on my forearms… a large power drill greeted me. Razor sharp drill bits and a wet rag flanked the tool. The cloth was drenched with a red substance. I was uneasy, shaken. My first thought was blood. Had there been an accident in this room? A worker? I didn't touch a thing. I decided the liquid could be red paint. I juggled the options in my head, all of them making sense for the moment, rational notions. But there were no red walls. No gallons of red paint anywhere in sight; nothing remotely close to red. I took a deep breath and kept my focus. The long hall wound around a corner to another wing. I passed a series of rooms, all of the doors closed. I took a few more strides and heard a crashing noise in a room behind me, followed by a creak. Something probably fell and hit a door, I told myself over and over again. A ladder, perhaps construction supplies on a shelf. I had to get to the roof and stop wasting time.

The next corridor put me at a stairwell. I felt a little disoriented, the layout was a bit more intricate compared to last time. The plaque on the door read "Stairs to Level 2." I was getting there. I climbed the stairs and hustled, leaping and covering three steps at a time. My footsteps echoed in the empty stairwell, the sound ricocheting from wall to wall. I braced my hand on the railing and sprung up the flight of stairs. The door I arrived at read "F2." I thrust it open but it almost immediately slammed shut behind me and left me in the center of a vast room with a high ceiling. Electrical wires dangled from holes in the wall. Sturdy, metal support beams were visible behind the framework of the ceiling tile. A ladder stood across the room with various hand tools, screwdrivers and such, hanging in the slots. A spackle bucket sat in front of the window to my left with tubes of caulk and the dispenser next to it.

A trace of light appeared in the room across the hall fifteen feet from me. Shelves in that room held various neatly organized supplies, lights shining down on them. The floor was comprised of interlocking walls, alcoves that wandered aimlessly into large offices. I could see water fountains here and there. Out of nowhere I heard a murky grunt. My heart skipped a beat.

What? What was that?

The noise was different than before, mysterious, unlike anything I've ever heard. The inhuman groan came from the other side of the wall. Blood channeled through my veins ice-cold. The sound intensified to an eerie pitch, a screech. Beads of sweat slid down my forehead. Was I hearing things? I gathered my bearings, tried to collect myself, and attempted to get the hell out of this labyrinth. I felt like I had stepped into a dark, dreary world in a matter of minutes; regaining my perspective, retracing my path, was nearly impossible unless I stopped my manipulative brain from feeding me those demons. Ten feet away was another path, a way out of the room, the trap. The set of double doors I saw seemed like a getaway. Relief washed over me, eased my fear. I felt a taste of adrenaline fire inside me. I ran to the doors. I encountered a janitor's closet with more suspicious evidence to examine. The faucet ran beyond a drip. Various bloody saw blades were scattered on top of the sink. Streams of chunky blood oozed into the drain. I flinched away. In the corner of the room a sledgehammer leaned against the wall, the steel head smeared with blood that dripped down the handle. Who did this? When? Was the perpetrator still around?

I left nothing to chance. I scampered over to the ladder and lifted a screwdriver from one of the slots. I was armed, desperate to find an escape, but aware of the clock ticking, precious seconds fleeting past. Better to abandon the mission of finding a roof hatch, and get out the quickest way. My pulse accelerated. I felt my heart pumping madly, the beat slapping my chest walls with vicious strokes. There was a bitter taste in my mouth, coppery and gritty, bone dry. Suddenly my cellular phone rang, startling me. I was hesitant to answer. Was this a game? I didn't want to play anymore. All logic eluded me, I answered it. Unnerving static thrashed in my ear.

Shshshshshshshshshshshshshshshshsh

I felt a presence in the room. I sensed eyes upon me, hawking my every step, every move, honing in on my thoughts. I felt its strength; its supernatural force brushed my shoulders and peppered my neck.

What does it want? What is it? A man? A monster?

I was desperate to catch my breath. I was lost, disoriented, wearing down quickly. My head was throbbing, thumping. It was as though someone was playing tug-of-war with my skull. I ran to the closest window and caught a glimpse of my co-workers on standby below. They were oblivious to my panic but at least seeing them lifted my spirits a bit. I pounded the glass with my fist five of six times. My dry knuckles busted open and bled. The guys couldn't hear me. Inside the room my hammering was loud, but on the outside almost inaudible, I assumed. I waved my arms in wild arcs, swinging them around, up and down, every way possible.

"Can't you guys see me god damn it?" I

shouted.

One of them luckily looked up while the rest were huddled in the distance. I saw two men, Tim and Chris.   Where was Evan?   Chris was pointing frantically at me, his finger fluttering, covered in orange safety gloves.   My arms were still flailing, questions still spinning inside of me.   Can he interpret my motions? Does he understand my silent call for help? The horrifying conclusion stared me in the face coldly. Whatever it was that had been tormenting me in the confines of Bayview was behind me. I had to face it.   Fight it.   No more dodging the inevitable.   I invoked my courage.   I clutched the screwdriver in my fist ready for defense; my forehead dripping with sweat.   I prepared myself to meet the fate in store for me.   I spun around with the screwdriver, raised it above my ear, poised to bear down. Nothing. No one. I stood frozen and scared. My eyes darted around the room and floated from one dark corner to the next. "Who are you? Where are you hiding?" I asked aloud.

I tore out of the room and made haste for an exit. As I scrambled for the nearest way out I met another set of stairs. I descended until my wobbly legs hit the lower half, propelling me with long strides to the bottom. When I crossed the room I realized it put me right back where the journey began, closer to escape. Yet another obstacle impeded my path. The door I entered earlier was shut. I had left it open before and the carpet was now soaked with blood. My feet stumbled over construction materials in the path of my escape. I got to the front door. It was jammed. Shit! Now what? This was too much, too hard to handle. I bolted to the far end of the room where a door was hidden behind a heating unit. I barreled through it to safety!

The perspiration on my face dried on contact with the freezing-cold temperature outdoors. The biting cold brought a puddle of tears to my eyes, flushed my face crimson with terror. When I met up with the crew I explained everything, hurriedly, I guess. All of them broke into laughter like they always did. "What was Chris pointing at?" I asked. "I saw him from the upstairs window." The guys were puzzled, they thought I was nuts.

"Where is Evan, that son of a bitch?" I said.

Scott tried to calm me down. "Easy man, take the day off or something, get your head together.

You're losing it."

A security guard drove up. When I asked where the hell he was during my run in with danger he looked confused. His eyes squinted and he turned away from me as the rest of them did. I didn't expect much from the guard. They're careless anyway, never in place when you need them, too afraid to confront a real threat, useless actually. Everyone parted ways and I strolled off the anxiety by heading to the bottom of the parking lot. The team was a distance ahead of me so I hung back a bit to clear my head. I grabbed a handkerchief from my pants pocket and wiped the cold moisture from my sockets. I blew my congested nose.

Out of nowhere I heard a pounding noise in back of me, a thud, hard and strong. The disturbance dared me to turn and look. I gave in to the urge, the test used up the last shreds of my courage. I spun around. The streetlamp overhead, about fifty feet away, illuminated a hulking shape in the upstairs window; the same one I punched earlier.

The thing I saw was enormous, its fingers like tentacles pressed against the pane of glass. It wore a hat, a sombrero of sorts, with clumps of hair spilling out from the brim. The man-thing stepped backwards and a small trail of light from the office glossed over its face. A mouthful of cracked teeth is what came forward in the light. They were metallic, sharp. I covered my face and recoiled in horror, as helplessly frightened as when I had been inside. I felt weak, like the blood was drained from my body.

How can this be? My hands trembled over my face, fingers spasmodic, uncontrollable. I removed my hands one final time to be sure, to understand what my mind registered.

That hideous thing I saw was no longer visible in the window.

What is happening? How is it possible to…?

The men were out of sight and had no interest in what I had gone through in that building or what I had seen in the window. I jogged up the long road and caught up to them.

I begged for sunrise.

Death Do Us Part

I will try and explain it.

I drove through a graveyard yesterday and saw an old man standing alone in the center of the premises. As my car approached he turned and watched me roll by. The place had a spectacular layout of ornate headstones and monuments that displayed a never-ending list of names of the deceased. From a distance the place is surreal, spectacular. It presents breathtaking images of a world that fascinates many who pass by. One plot seems to flow into another. There are thousands of names engraved on the thousands upon thousands of tombstones. Flowers are exquisitely planted by loved ones who pay their respects, shedding tears of joy, or sorrow, depending on the memories that channel through them. The layouts are carved and crafted with precision, the tombs poised beautifully above the ground. I can't imagine how much time something so extraordinary could take to construct; an amount impossible to fathom ...Only death could bring that staggering answer.

I looked at the man, who couldn't have been a hair under seventy, and wondered. Was he the caretaker? I seriously doubted it. It was the droopy texture to his eyes that sent me an ambiguous message. He was wearing nice, clean clothes, a black fedora, shiny burgundy shoes, and a pair of bulky glasses. He walked, stared, then weaved in and out of every plot with care, purposefully studying the stones as if he knew every single occupant that was six feet under.

It was a chilling sight. He was not fazed at all by my presence and he continued to go about his business, whatever it was, with a calm that stunned me. He kept removing his glasses, rubbing his eyes, then replacing them. Little tidbits started to freak me out. Did he know the people that were buried there? It's fair to say that he passed at least two dozen stones and studied each meticulously. I watched from the end of the driveway that divided the cemetery in half. I could've left, but I was amazed by his eccentricities. Never in my life have I seen a human act in that manner. Sure, maybe he was passing through. Maybe he was paying respects to a loved one and was walking off his grief. Perhaps he was told he had little time to live and he wanted to see how it all ends. Regardless, his actions disturbed the hell out of me. But I never felt threatened by him. After all, my best guess would put him in the neighborhood of seventy, seventy five years old. I decided to drive away and come back later that night. I drove around all alone grasping for answers to what I perceived as a mystery worth solving alone. A good three hours must have passed before I returned and pulled into the cemetery once more to bear witness to the strange, elderly man. Surely he walked past hundreds of the burial shrines while I was gone...maybe more. I drove up the hill and proceeded all the way to the back of the lot on the prowl for him. I turned onto the rear service road and came to a stop. I waved my flashlight in every possible direction searching for him but...

He was gone.

Upon closer inspection I saw something in the

back corner of the grounds, tucked away, sequestered in the final row. A lantern was glowing. Shadows danced on the nearby dingy wooden fence. I raced up to the flickering light and my heart palpitated faster and stronger in my chest. The black fedora was resting neatly on top of his burgundy shoes, glasses stuffed inside them. Dirt was piled high in front of a blank tombstone with a shovel staking down a piece of paper. I picked it up and read the print.

I kept my promise to you, Bernice, my love. I will find you soon so I can love you forever, or die trying.

Walter.

Biography

Since David was just a kid he was a fan of everything horror. He enjoyed the adrenaline rush of a good scare, and one day hoped to find a creative outlet within the realms of the genre. This book is his first stab at unleashing the most frightening tales from the darkest depths of his imagination. David resides in Denville, N.J. with his wife Elizabeth. You can learn more about him by visiting, www.myspace.com/davidbfear.

CPSIA information can be obtained at www.ICGtesting.com
Printed in the USA
BVOW070253151012

302898BV00001B/2/P